Dingle ~

Hope there exists
something of the equality
between Man and Nature between
those lines - as told to me by
The Old Man of The Sea.

Best wishes

Rupert

LPR La Prensa Rebelde

Europe - Havana - The Americas - The East

...of dark voices on salt air

A NOTE ON THE AUTHOR

Rupert Mould was born in North America. During his teens he settled in England with his mother and sister. He read a BA Hons. in Spanish and English Literature, then a MPhil in Modern Poetry at Stirling University, Scotland. His first book was 'The Rebel Radio Diary'. He lives in Bristol, England and Zahara de la Sierra, al-Andalus, Spain. He is 31 years old. Speaks French, Spanish and English and owns an XT 500 motorcycle.

Edited by, **Steve Henwood** - Moonson Co.

Published by, 'la prensa rebelde - LPR'.

Cover artwork and illustrations, **Jenny Whiskerd**.
Fisherman image, Laida Perez Blaya.

First issued with 'The Cuban Master Sessions Series, Calle 23, Havana'.
Commercially released by 'Ninja Tune Records', London, England and
Montreal, Canada.
Albums released in two parts throughout the years 2000 - 2001.

ISBN 0-9538553-1-7

Cover layout and typesetting by haydn.suckling@blueyonder.co.uk
Book printers, Creative Print And Design Group, Blaenau Gwent, Wales.

Visit the 'Up, Bustle and Out' website for regular updates, film
footage, further information on 'LPR' publications, press reactions, our
exciting and latest recordings in the making, concert info, literary criti-
cisms, photographic exhibition, other links to 'Ninja Tune' / 'Canadian
Powder Tours' / 'Zahara de la Sierra', music and fantasy - all at:

http://www.upbustleandout.co.uk
e: rebel.radio@blueyonder.co.uk

   'Peaceful in the desert, rebels in the crowd'
   'The smokeyness of Bristol, the coolness of Havana'

'Up, Bustle and Out' have recorded 5 albums for 'Ninja Tune Records' -
The Breeze Was Mellow As The Guns Cooled In the Cellar / One Colour
Just Reflects Another / Light 'Em Up, Blow 'Em Out / The Cuban Master
Sessions 1 & 2, Calle 23, Havana.

To view an unabashed embrace of revolutionary politics as featured in
the 'Miami New Times' go to:
http://www.miaminewtimes.com/issues/2000-09-07/kulchur.html.

Many thanks to:

Clandestine Ein, Steve Henwood for his long hours and skills editing this work, Gemma for typing the scrawling manuscript, Haydn for detail to artwork, Emmanuel Georges, Cristóbal Herrera Ulashkevich - photographer, 'K-Industria' team in Barcelona for licensing this Series throughout Spain, The English Department of the University of Stirling, Scotland, Martin Genge, Andy Hague, Jim Barr, Keith Warmington, John Donegan, Jules 'Shoes' Elvins of 'Waldo Films', London, 'LA CAFÉ' Film Crew, NYC:

Alom Tissé, FelizP, Fader and Professor Uncle Díaz, Jenny Whiskerd, Mr. Miles Essex + Xavier for CD-ROM to 'Sessions 1', 'La Radio Rebelde Crew in La Habana, Cuba, 'Ninja Tune Records' - London and Montreal, mi pueblo arabe 'Zahara de la Sierra', al-Andalus, España, los albañiles Diego 'El Revolucionario del Sofa', Tani, Juan Pablo 'El Quinto', el maestro Juan – 'ioh, me da mucha pena trabajar asi!', el jefe José Pincoa – 'El Frances', Laida Perez Blaya, John Evan Rogers for advice and detail to printing, the spirit and writings of Alexander Von Humboldt, T. S. Eliot, Edward Brathwaite, Arundhati Roy for 'The God of Small Things', Ernest Hemingway's influential little book 'The Old Man And The Sea', 'The Revelation' of St. John The Divine, I B Micheal for his inspiring book 'prince', Micheal Ondaatje for 'The English Patient', Poets John Ashbery, Langston Hughes, Pablo Neruda and W. B. Yeats, Joseph Conrad, The Cuban people for what they have opposed and have come to represent in the history of poor countries seeking Respect and Independence, Señorita Yilian Cruz Meadón, Gregorio Fuentes – The Original Old Man Of The Sea, Sally and Susan Mould, Grandma H, Ralph, Frances Vesma for great artwork, the memories of those that fought fascism in the Spanish Civil War – respect, My greatest friend 'Abuela Bab', Ben Kinnaird for time on website designs, Miss Jaipall Bagh – The 'J. B. E' in a bug, Mr 'P', Marco - rent of laptop, Gunjen on sensibility, Big Al + Duncan – 'The Reggae Jammers', Tania who mentioned Humboldt to me, Sarah and Juan de las Abejas, Nick and Matt - 'Los Muchachos de Manchester', DJ Danny, Andy Kershaw + Mary Anne Hobbs for playing our music on Radio 1, UK, Susanna Glaser + Neil of Muzik Magazine, Bristol's Venue Magazine for great support – especially Nige Tassell, La belle Madmoiselle Parmentier et sa famille, Querida amiga Eugenia Ledesma, David Muñoz del Pino, the rather aloof science of Loren Eiseley and 'The Immense Journey', Laurie Lee, Sally @ Zzonked Promotions, Simon @ Impress, Eileen @ Primary Talent Agency for bookings, Brock Phillips, Brett Sokol of 'The Miami New Times' newspaper, Journalists Jon Wesley and Mike Wolf, 'Julia Hill' and 'The Circle of Life Foundation' for her/their tremendous courage protecting old forests from the US multinational logging companies, all the artists and musicians that have worked with us wholeheartedly over the last 10 years – all of You who have supported us. Gracias queridos compañeros - sigamos creciendo y luchando...

The Day The Prince Came...

...deeply veiled in meaning He,
the forlorn Prince of outstanding grace,
whose secret sorrows embrace a tide,
that is forever rising and touching,
washing in wild whispers of mere being,
His memories that shift with the shingle,
to and fro—are the motions of any day.

Nature treats him as an equal;
equally merciless,
the Sea, colder in rising,
seems blacker than blue somehow,
breaking gently his bare bones,
against the rocks where,
marooned, He dreams in prayer;
His moods succumb to the Muse*

She beckons so sweetly,
at this moment of making,
in reverie he does not see outside himself;
battered like a religion upon a barren rock,
this exact rock that holds his nakedness,
to sleep whilst standing upon soles,
that work precisely to keep him there, until—

He awakes to a Sea caressing his thighs,
surprised by his reaction,
He cups his hands round nothingness and shouts,
shouts fly back at him from—
from where exactly?
Somewhere over, nowhere,
but they return in waves,
slapping him in the face 'til white,
so beautifully bone white—like—
An Angel chiselled out of a block of salt...

* a goddess that inspires a creative artist, esp. a poet.

...monumental in white crystals upon blue,
he makes his fragile permanent stand,
estranged but to his passions and pains,
that blister the Sea's glazed mirror,
foretelling of his fate.

An arcane World awaits;
sky and Sea play for keeps,
upon the films of his eyes,
both encircle his sensitive nape,
teasing wet and dry tongues—sensually,
Dishing-out mortal desires.

No panic grips him,
not a single quiver of fear,
aloft his clenched fist defines,
the will of his people who now call him d
                                        o
                                        w
                                        n.

L—ovingly;
    one wave kissed his lips.

O—pium sweetly;
     the next perfumed his lungs.

S—trangely;
    the next whispered in his ears.

T—ruthfully;
    the next confessed all whilst,
    combing his hair and leading him there

Oct' 1998.

Preamble

It was during April, May and June 1998 we were invited to record a 'Master Sessions Series' in Havana, Cuba. 'Part 1' was released on July 10th 2000 with a docu-drama film and book.

'Part 1', through the book - The Rebel Radio Diary, details how and why this series developed, along with defining the implications and message incorporated in its release: the US-led trade embargo enforced on Cuba is illegal, the Cuban nation has a strong rhythmic and historical vitality, and that Cuba is widely seen as a deep source of hope for other poor countries looking to ascertain their independence.

We couldn't have ignored these fundamental issues whilst recording, writing and filming this series - we heard them in the studio, as echoes in the streets, saw them as vibrant wall murals, debated them in University buildings and on street corners.

It came as no shock that the Miami Press Agencies contacted our own. For all the heated debating, the surprises really came after the Miami New Times ran our story in a long feature article. Shortly after publication we were striking up correspondences with Latin Americans and American-born Cubans. We came together over the tense right-wing politics of Miami and then moved away towards the fresher mentality of the people in cities like Mexico and New York.

From out of New York City came a talented ensemble called LA CAFÉ, who had filmed some startling scenes from rooftops all across Havana. Their 15-minute film, directed by Juan Carlos Alom, is called 'Habana Solo'. Señor Franklin J. Díaz posted us a copy. We watched some very moving Black and White footage that captured precisely our moods and intentions for the Master Sessions Series. We loved their work so much that we asked to license it for the CD-ROM on Part 2. They came back with a better suggestion - they would film fresh footage on Super 8 film in Spanish Harlem, NYC and then return to Havana to capture some new images. A great and welcome addition to 'Master Sessions 2'.

Just pop the CD into your computer.

By looking back on the correspondence, the project achieved far more than we had ever imagined. To have sensed some of the spirit of South America and to have been accepted by them in this way has always been one of my creative ambitions since we cut our first record in 1990. UB&O are all aware that the second album in a series is rarely received as warmly and enthusiastically as the first. Yet we believe that this shouldn't be the case.

'Sessions 2' holds as much flavour musically, visually and in literature as the first, and it is not a mirror reflection. The filmmakers are different, the book a complete departure from the first, as is the studio technique and equipment that we used to produce these songs. We have maintained the flow between Havana, Cuba and Bristol, England.

The 'Cuban Master Sessions Series' signifies great hope and great fun, tense creative emotions stored during the many years of studying history, literature, the Cuban Descarga, and the experiences of other famous visitors such as Graham Greene, Ernest Hemingway, Salvador Allende and, of course, the ubiquitous hero Che Guevara. Equally, it carries a searching voice rooted in history and spiced with direct observations made through the Aperture of Youth during our work in the Havana studio 'Sonocaribe', at 'Radio Rebelde' and encountered whilst travelling the Island.

'...of dark voices on salt air' digresses from the immediacy of direct observation and adopts a story. No Socialist Revolution, just an uncomplicated backdrop of a white beach, an open Sea, an outcrop of rock and an old Cuban Fisherman.

The Fisherman washes up on a brilliant beach having survived a terrific battle with a courageous fish and the punishment of a cruel and wracking storm. He is weakened both physically and mentally, beyond the point where instinct could build himself up again.

Introspection consumes his limited time. His challenges are now spiritual – he's occupied in the piecing together of meanings and questions relating to tradition, freedom, history, journeying, isolation and community. A great number of voices are heard, and from many arcane sources such as the Sea, flotsam and jetsam, a manikin, his own mind's trickery, his people, his family, nature, Gods, horizons...

Many visions fuel his quest for the meaning of his lifetime spent upon the Sea.

Tradition makes him proud of who he is, how he lives and the community with whom he shares his experiences.

A distant blackness hangs in the northern sky. It is of a sweeping uniformity. He never fully comprehends its significance, other than it troubles him, believing that it threatens his community. His thoughts become a Poetry of Protection.

One hot and sticky afternoon, as we were laying down a Descarga in Estudio Sonocaribe, the trumpet maestro Juan Larrinaga told me, in passing, that he had known Ernest Hemingway, and that he had been over to his house in San Francisco de Paula. He also spoke of outings at Sea with Hemingway in his boat, moored at Cojímar.

It was another hot afternoon when that North American writer met an old Fisherman in Cojímar, who was to become the central figure of his book 'THE OLD MAN AND THE SEA'. This came as great news to me. In 1995 whilst studying for a BA in Literature my mother gave me that short novel, inscribed 'Hope this little book will help you with your writing'. For my mother, the book's charm was immortalised in short and structurally simple sentences that carried much philosophical depth. It concerned struggle. Life is often a struggle.

Cojímar was the fishing village where this novel was set. Miraculously, the old fisherman still lives his daily village life although no longer pushing out to Sea. This I discovered when I met him. Everyone knew of him. The Sea breeze whispered his name, the *Palmas Reales* *1 rustled their leaves in sentences extracted from the book, the deck planking of the moored fishing boats creased speaking the Words: 'El Viejo, El Viejo, El Viejo'.

Leaving Havana on foot along a quiet hot road is an odd thing to do. Not solely due to the heat, but more to do with the weird way a capital city just peters out, leaving rubbish to fall over as the only signs of mass human population - bottles, tins, discarded papers, worn tyres, chairs.... The road passes right through the heart of Habana del Este where the block apartments become replaced by level plains that border the Sea. You hear the nearby wash of the Sea and the hiss off the road as the heat rises. Suddenly, the capital just seems to give up, remains still, brick by brick it refuses to follow. The city buzz is contained within its walls and gets left behind. The overpowering urban rhythm is replaced by a calmer pattern that is closer to the workings of nature. You begin to think differently.

I had reckoned on the walk being 20 kilometres. It wasn't - only about 12. And the time passed quickly; the constant presence, noise and attraction of the Sea overwhelmed any thoughts about the distance and heat.

The shoreline was strangely non-picturesque with rock and earthy banks, yet the Sea sparkled with a silvery-blue and the waves broke cleanly upon the point where you see the land to an end. The silver glints were so strong that they were blinding. My eyes tricked me, making me believe that I could still see sparkles that had long since gone. I could see silver in blue, silver in the black of my mind.

Echoes of T. S. Eliot's The Four Quartets... I could hear the music of his poem carried on the stillness of a wave's back, in its restless crashing over the shoreline. Eliot's major poem is embedded into this story. His poems have smuggled meanings into my work and affected the character of it; the images of a menacing 'old crab with barnacles on its back gripping the end of a stick', the moon having 'lost her memory', and 'smiling into corners'. And also 'the prayer of the bone on the beach' - all have claimed me as the reader, as I have taken private ownership of the poems. For a moment we had a cryptic relationship. I tuned my ears to those many 'voices of the Sea' and to the 'whine in the rigging' until I began to discover that there was indeed something very musical with feeling and with language waiting.

I caught sight of a small working skiff out at Sea, manned by a solitary figure. In many ways, the Old Man's tale made Hemingway famous. It was such a simple one: an Old Fisherman, a lifetime hunting at Sea, his vulnerability through old age, contrasting with the agelessness and strength of the Sea. There was equally the macho act of killing a big fish. Then that big fish took on grander proportions, more respect; its fight was also killing the Old Man. He suddenly realises that he is only better, stronger than the fish through trickery, and this affects his pride.

Hemingway wrote:

He took all his pain and what was left of his strength and his long-gone pride and he put it against the fish's agony and the fish came over onto his side and swam gently on his side, his bill almost touching the planking of the skiff, and started to pass the boat, long, deep, wide, silver and barred with purple and interminable in the water. *2

The reader can really sense the struggle, the lassitude, the relationship between the hunter and the hunted. Both had to fight to beyond the point where victory and defeat haven't any meaning. But there is a respect present in the act of dying - the Old Man acknowledges this. The fish's

colour and size have the aura and magnitude of the Sea. And what does a person truly possess after a long lifetime but a skeleton of experience?
A fantastic story of great meaning.

When I spotted that solitary figure afloat on the Sea's openness in such a small vessel, I remembered how I, as a boy in the Americas, would often face the Sea and think 'even if I was to one day become a big person, I would always be small here'.

Hemingway knew that. T. S. Eliot knew that:

We cannot think of a time that is oceanless.   *3

I turned my gaze inwards. Nearer the shore where I saw a largish outcrop of rock: old strata from the beginnings of time, trapped between the origins of life at Sea and the fundamentals of life on land. The story was already forming around the solitary floating figure, the openness of the Sea, the solitude of his tradition, the branding voices of history, and by the great poets before me who wrote of the Sea's 'many voices' and 'many gods'. Through them I began to hear and see my own.
    Alexander Von Humboldt wrote in his wonderful way and his inspiring book PERSONAL NARRATIVE OF A JOURNEY TO THE EQUINOCTIAL REGIONS OF THE NEW CONTINENT:

How strangely mobile is man's imagination, eternal source of his joys and pains! *4

Also:

Limitless space suggests higher matters, and elevates the minds of those who enjoy solitary meditation. *5

To develop a sense of 'limitless space' and isolation, I went by boat and motorcycle to the Outer Hebrides Islands. There I camped on white Caribbean-esque beaches in near 24 hours of summertime, Northern-Hemisphere daylight, exposed to the wild weather and to the omnipresent powers of loneliness and imagination. 'Limitless space' did make me think deeper and harder into abstraction. But the enjoyment of solitary meditation requires more than a setting.

Further along the Cuban coast, beauty in the clothes of nature and man's presence fashioned themselves before me. The Palmas Reales that had caught the admiration of Alexander Von Humboldt grew out of the sand, notched like ladder rungs and bent right over, as if tilting their ears towards the Sea's consonants. I stood on a plain plank bridge and saw a colourful skiff lashed by rough rope to a bank. There was an Old Man resting on the skiff's capping beams at the tiller, a fair-sized Marlin was laid out along the planking. I thought it must have been an honorary statue - but no, this was for real. I was approaching the little village called Cojímar, bringing myself closer to the person and the events that comprise that award-winning story.

Cojímar is so very sleepy, clean and picturesque. It owes its existence to the Sea, many of the village men wrestle with her to make a living. There wasn't a car in sight or sound. Boats of numerous forms and sizes littered the beach and harbour. There were many colours bouncing off the white and gold backdrop.

The fishermen were already back and settling down to an afternoon at the bar. The bar was very much different to any in Havana that I had been in. There weren't any bottles with foreign labels on the shelves. Here it was cool Cuban beer, backyard rum no doubt, then maybe a Mojito with luck, coffee, canned drinks, a tasty coffee liqueur, or, the inevitable Agua Sagrada! - Holy Water!

There was also less wall decoration, less overall commercial character - as one would expect. Just white walls, wooden tables and chairs where sat dark-skinned bristly men - tokers of home-rolled cigars, observing the afternoon taking shape. Their faces showed an attractive starkness, like the very Sea they worked. Their eyes seemed deep set - fathoms deep, netting mysteries and wise experiences. Many had unusual facial lines accentuated by the sun and wind, almost smooth, desert-like, yet patterned in waves by nature's courses.

In front of the bar door was a small plaza constructed around a white bust of Hemingway. He had a strong round face with many lines too - only his were seeping with runs of rusty iron, like sun-baked blood. His eyes had that rather sad shape about them when eyes droop at their outer ends. A serious man, beyond his brutish look, he was also kind and caring. There was also a sense of fun, making it harder to imagine that he shot himself rather than face a hapless battle with cancer.

He wrote so intimately of a struggle and the pain of deprivation, yet when faced with a futile battle himself, he decided to end it all before its natural conclusion. May be the Fish would have ended its struggle sooner if it

didn't think it had a fighting chance, or if it hadn't understood what the old man understood:

You are killing me, fish, the old man thought. But you
have a right to. Never have I seen a greater, or more
beautiful, or a calmer or more noble thing than you,
brother. Come on and kill me. I do not care who kills
who. *6

As I viewed the bust from within the bar, a voice by the
side of me repeated in heavily accented Spanish-English,
   'Hemingway. Ernesto Hemingway.'
   Suddenly the whole bar area seemed to echo with the
Words 'El Viejo Y El Mar'.
   I was told that 'El Viejo', Gregorio Fuentes, 'está senta-
do allí' - was sitting over there.
   He must have been in his late 90s.
   Our eyes momentarily met. His were discoloured,
creamy, ghostly.
   The noise of the bar suddenly receded and the waves
returned whispering:

   'El Viejo'
   'El Mar'
   'El Viejo'
   'El Mar'
   'El Viejo'
   'El Mar'

...of dark voices on salt air

To the people of Cuba and their struggles

'We may only eat rice and beans for dinner, but we eat them happy.'

The sea is the land's edge also, the granite
Into which it reaches, the beaches where it tosses
Its hints of earlier and other creation:
The starfish, the horseshoe crab, the whale's backbone;
The pools where it offers to our curiosity
The more delicate algae and the sea anemone.
It tosses up our losses, the torn seine,
The shattered lobsterpot, the broken oar
And the gear of foreign dead men. The sea has many voices,
Many gods and many voices.

(T. S. Eliot, The Dry Salvages, The Four Quartets) *7

The Sea rose gently up, washing past the exhausted limbs of the old Fisherman, then filtering down through the polished grains of time. It was a defeat; a soul that had given its all to the openness of the Sea, a man that had struggled through to a self-respect so unique, now lay tired and torn on a bleached shore.

This shore, so brilliantly bone-white, bore witness to history - an immediate history like the old man's, also a cruel and romantic one that staged dark deeds, flickering at night like a lighthouse behind whose warnings lay exposed dreams.

Here the Sea has two faces: one that glistens with each ray of light, the other darkened to the pitch-black memory of extreme solitude.

The Fisherman lay unconscious, grounded between the blackness of defeat and the light of dreams by the gentle presence of breaking waves. Each one came differently. Each one broke speaking fragments of the same language.

The first three spoke,

'Bring in your net.'

'Brother, bring in your net.'

'Already the moon is out, and you'll not have time to get it in.'

The Fisherman stirred. The movement sent blood racing to his head. His mouth twisted at the corners and the deep rhythmic Words pushed through the crystallised salt that had set across his lips.

'Yes, I will bring in the net. I must do it soon, before the moon, much before the high moon. I work this net, work this Sea, as they work me. One knot tying many strings.'

More warm waves rose but the Fisherman's senses drifted to colder regions where ice flowers on crystal bergs are brushed by terrible winds. He had to grasp the subtle messages carried on these waves or release his grip on the net that was carved into his clenched hands.

Much later the voices came again,

'The sun, now young and strong.'

'Has defeated the moon.'

'That now leaves this very scene.'

'And so Hermano, will you cast or bring in your net?'

He began to surface from the darkened depths. Again he stirred a leg, then this time the other. A shiver chased through his limbs as a trickle of urine ran into the sand.

'Your net,' repeated a voice.

'Yes. Now, I will do it. I will bring it in. Who speaks to me in this way?'

The Fisherman eased open his eyelids and was struck by a blue sky that was still reddened with the soft orange of dawn. The moon was retreating not advancing. His first thought was of his suffering that he had borne out at Sea: the incessant pull of the line across his shoulders, the line running out across his leathery palms, and coiled, gaining depth on the fish. Those feelings of imminent victory. It had been a big fish and a proud one: a true fighter like himself.

That had been the third day.

A sudden shock of fatigue brought the fourth night closing in around him like the closing of dusty old hardback covers as sleep overcomes the last sentence of the night.

Then turbulence, deep eddies way out at Sea where a

concentration of elemental forces had been brewing. They approached, slowly at first but with a certainty, like rumbles on the wind from an advancing cavalry. So far out to Sea, three days of battle with a fighter fish, no harbour lights in sight or other vessels, overcome by a deep lassitude that was somehow closely connected to his very existence.

He was old and needed this last big catch.

He had known and survived worse storms. But his strength was failing and he couldn't sail away from that. From the deep dark of the Sea he had felt a fear that froze him, from the invisible depths where scavengers scuttled across sunken decks of rotting hulls, feeding off history's lies. It was as if in his very person he was somehow complicit, partly responsible for the visions that were sent from below to the infinite channels of his mind. It was haunting.

Sometimes he would lean over the capping beams to absorb the change of time by night. Often his reflection was stolen for a moment, distorted by the glint of a star. At that black moment he would see an eye, he called it the eye of the Sea, focusing on him. He would look directly into this eye and beyond it. He knew that at night there existed a dimension that could overthrow him. For this reason he always recited a prayer before pushing his skiff out to Sea; a few poetic Words here, a splash of rum there, a symbol traced into the air with his forefinger, and a second's pause before the ceremony was closed.

The other fishermen valued him as a part of the community but considered him strange, slightly apart. He made them uneasy. This uneasiness really started the day he stopped drinking a couple of beers with them after the nets were all in. Out at Sea late one night. The Fishermen were all grouped close, each one's position lit by oil lamps. As usual the old man peered over the edge and sought the eye.

Looking.

Always looking.

And the Sea gave way to a symbol of itself.

He was standing at the bar with his fellow pescadores, the same cloudy cigar-cell that stole so much of their lives. There entered a small boy, completely unknown to them. His skin glistened with many colours like a wet palace rooftop of coloured tiles. The light burst through the door after him like it was his friend racing to catch him up. Together they danced between the dust particles. The boy had an unusual manner about him.

The fishermen weren't accustomed to strangers. There was silence. Then the biggest brute amongst them walked up to the boy and stubbed a burning cigar out on his neck. A roar of laughter took hold of the crowd; madness enveloped the bar and all of them began hurling spit at him. Suddenly the Fisherman saw himself also spitting and laughing.

He dashed his hands out of the Sea and squatted on his heels with his back against the bottom boards and side planking of his skiff. The sharp movement shut off the random joys of the phosphorescent plankton that danced around his arms in the night water. But he was safely away from the mysteries of the edge.

The phosphorescence dispersed, the light drew into itself.

The eye of the Sea retreated into the deep blackness. A horrible vision. From then on, he felt the need to bring himself closer to the Sea, as if there had been a very long misunderstanding. He felt the desire to listen more sharply to the Sea.

Spiritually he had always been different from his fellow pescadores. He felt differently about this labour of isolation. Regrouping on the shore was odd to him after the long open-ended hours spent at Sea. He had feelings beyond the Words of the bar that they would not be able to share. His silence estranged him but taught him more about himself. He was more often alone and adrift on thoughts and so very small against a mighty backdrop.

Aside from the Sea and his family little else mattered.

At times he also believed that the Sea was showing him a map that unfolded as he peered down into the darkness. He would recognise certain places, including his Island, then struggle with other names and weird alphabetical juxtapositions.

Memories.

He had given up the fight in the swells, relinquished the line from across his shoulders, lost his balance, fallen against his skiff's timbers and then tossed and turned with each wave's strike. He remembered it all now. And the relief of having succumbed. He had borne the sufferings of the great Fish he had been fighting, he had accepted defeat to the power of the elements. The Sea had judged them both, awarded them equally and reasserted the fear amongst those who make a living from her. He fell unconscious upon a sleepless Sea.

Mercy, never a Word muttered at a time of greater meaning.

May he rest in peace upon his Sea.

Blue. Blue. Blue.

This was the only colour in view as he began to roll his head. The Sea chased up his legs and pooled around his crotch. The sun was rising warm, the morning still after the storm.

The Fisherman and his skiff were as two pieces of drift-wood beached low upon bleached sand. They were in a little inlet guarded by eighty-foot Palmas Reales. The heavy leaves pointing rigidly upwards, stiff in the flirtation of a moderate breeze – una brisa suave. The tops of the trees shone with a tender green, the spearhead tips were leathery. The younger petioles contrasted with the white fissured older ones. A bird clung to a stem, its tail low, its head held high. It didn't ruffle a feather perched upon its throne, at peace and reflective like a revered Majesty of Colour – *La Majesdad del Color.*

Now the colours were flooding in like the blood in his awakened veins. With all the perceptions ached his hunger, his thirst.

The Fisherman clumsily pulled himself up onto his elbows. The effort opened recent wounds. A length of netting line had sunk into his left palm, carved deep from the struggle and set hard in his dried blood. He winced as the movement forced it out of his palm. The dried blood cracked, opening up fissures for the fresh blood to flow like a desert riverbed after rainfall from some distant place. He traced the various scars etched into his palms - old stories.

His skiff lay side-on only three metres away, rocking with each wave. Its name - Eleanora - flashing like a roughly-cut film between frames. Then the angle changed as another wave brought it further towards him. On the bottom boards he saw storm water swilling around and a packet of cigarettes. He read the mark "Fortuna" with the Words "Sabe a ti" written below.

'But what fortune knows of me? mused the Fisherman.

'Enough old man, bring in the line, then the net will follow.'

Once upon his feet the Fisherman began coiling his line but without the usual practised smoothness. He looped it over a batten protruding above the boat's stem. The hook was gone, the fight lost. He reached below the bows where his fifteen-litre water drum fitted tight like a grand encyclopaedia volume. There was little water left considering the size of the container, but sufficient. His thirst eased almost immediately.

'Bueno!' he exclaimed, 'let's have a look where I am.'

The *Majesdad del Color* fluttered from high up on the palm. His attentive beady black eyes cocked at forty-five degrees to observe this strange newcomer.

'I have nothing to offer you, your most highly positioned Majesty. Only these scraps of fish, though I ought really to keep them for myself. You have your wonderful Kingdom. Just fly and everything is under your command. Sorry, I am rude, ruined, unsure of myself just now.'

The old man turned away, reached for the net and began to haul it in. He braced himself to spread the tension, pulled and nearly fell backwards with the ease at which it started to come in.

'The net surely is cut, lost. Too light, far too light. A terrible storm.'

When most of it lay around him he handled it with greater delicacy, like nimble fingers strumming harp strings. The net rubbed against the stern as it came in with a string-like tone that changed ever so slightly as its speed varied - almost like a tired bow over a cello.

'I am foolish to be doing this at seventy-six years of age! I am tormented, trapped between treason and loyalty, my loyalty to the Sea. I feel like the devoted servant forced to depart from the source of his love and loyalty: my memories are so beautiful, beautiful and melancholy.'

The net was now fully in and bundled on the sand. The Fisherman took the final corner in his hand and walked away, stretching it out as he went. He did this to all the corners until it was fully extended.

'Beautiful? Melancholy?'

'Who said that?'

The old man was as if nailed on the grainy spot of his Paradise Lost. The *Majesdad del Color* looked down, head still cocked at a forty-five degree angle.

'Did you hear that voice?' he asked the bird.

He could no longer remember the moment when he first started hearing the voices, talking with them. In the days spent alone at Sea one's own company became a real companion along with the winds, the waves, the flotsam and jetsam, the catches.

'I am defeated,' sighed the old man. 'I know this will be my final place'

'You mutter meaningless Words, Fisherman.'

The old man turned towards the breaking waves. These voices were a part of him, rising from somewhere within him.

'Surely not entirely meaningless?' he began. '

He rapidly opened and closed his sore hand where the groove of the line had cut into him. The pain flashed within him and he hoped the biting sensation would settle the voices down.

The sun was now up and moving. Beads of sweat escaped his thick clumps of black-grey hair. He brushed his forearms over his forehead, lay down and tried to push aside the gnawing hunger. Words were spilling over him, thoughts swamping him and trapping his will. He felt once again like a child being instructed that life was made up of a density of information and that he would forever be learning. He sat hopelessly as these great lessons were being whispered from somewhere beyond his reach.

'Meaningless Words are Victory and Defeat. Life is above these events and images. We must present new ones. Victory drains a people - a cause is won, then soon lost as a strong desire is replaced by the everyday. The Defeat that you experience now is perhaps the closest that you have come to a true Victory.'

This voice hung in the air. He felt certain this time that it had come from somewhere other than himself. It was challenging and purer.

The Fisherman needed to think clearly, to locate food, water and to repair his boat. But he was preoccupied.

'So, if victory weakens a people, then the greatest victory one can achieve must be the narrowest of defeats. Like this the desire is kept smouldering, the inspiration to keep trying, to bring about change and.... Is this right what you say? Do I interpret it well?'

The waves broke heavily, the leaves of the Palmas Reales soaked up sun and rustled like grass skirts worn by dancers. The sand shifted ominously along. These continu-

al musical noises faded into the background, into silence.
Absolute silence.

He woke to further discomfort - the sun.

The brilliance penetrated the darkness of his closed eyes.
He rose and went over to his skiff and succeeded in dragging it up a further inch or two. On deck there were dried
cuts of dolphin and Peces Golondrinos - Flying Fish. He put
a morsel of dolphin to his mouth but couldn't stomach the
staleness of the flesh and the rancid smell. Although he
was a Fisherman he rarely ate fish. He loved fishing for the
tradition; the stories that he had heard. He had quickly discovered an occult poetry at Sea. Such an uncertain
romance he had never found in the big city, although he
loved the bright lights and the chrome on the cars glinting
like capped teeth in clandestine mouths. He loved more the
thousands of different shades of blue that made up the sky
and the Sea; the minute variations over such huge expans-
es mixed with his vulnerability and uncertainty. These subtle shades expressed his character.

Whenever a life was lost at Sea he would hear the villagers' lament. He grew more determined to make Her love
him, spare him the wrath that took others. His love was
deep. He never took the Sea for granted.

There was also his admiration for the life that existed
below the surface upon which was supported his own.
Although he killed, he felt no superiority, despite the hero-
ic stories that lingered in the streets - his Grandfather had
secured the biggest single catch ever, had become a leg-
end through his dignified death.

On other occasions he would thrust the harpoon into the

fish's body and hold on tight to the end absorbing the twists, feeling the pain that soon would kick and pass. The bloodied Sea would prevent eyes meeting. The big catches often sped off though speared and hooked, trailing blood as they swam but preferring clear water in which to sink to a more private World. These kills he hated. The brilliant colours of the scales, the purple that faded into grey before him. Greyness and death go hand in hand. With his greyness had come a loss of dexterity, an obvious sapping of his strength supported by harder and older wearing features. He admired the contrasts between life in the Sea and life on the land. Even more so when he learned that all life on land originated at Sea.

Wild Blue Majesty he called her - *La Majesdad del Azul Salvaje* and the people of the pueblo had so loved this term that they named the only bar after it, after Her. He had been pleased at this until the voices came. Then he wanted it changed, as if disrespectful somehow to the Sea.

On the Island his liberty was challenged - there were other commitments and obligatory traditions. At Sea he was free like revolutionary free verse poetry. The only protection he sought was through the strength of love. The Sea was his poetry of protection, his Island was condemned to history's failure and greed. He could never understand why he would be tormented by images of rotting hulls and scavengers picking up ruined fragments from the Seabed.

Now he was beached on the whitest, purest space that he had ever seen.

'She would not have taken my life. This I should have known,' he confirmed.

He glanced at his net - stiff and dry like his throat, then

at his boat, swollen like his stomach.
The voices crept up on him and began again to announce
their presence,

When I was hungry, you fed me books,
Now I am thirsty, you would stone me with syllables,
We seek, we seek,
But find no one to speak,
The Words to save us,
Search,
Forever in troubled silence,

There is no destination,
Our prayers reach.   *8

The Fisherman shrugged his shoulders and turned his gaze
toward his boat and the film edits of Eleanora - the com-
ings and goings, moving towards him and away in mean-
ingful rhythms.
'Just as she did twenty years ago,' he remembered and
reached for a batten out of his skiff with which to score the
sand.

'So you think that you can write in this state, do you Fisherman? That you can create?'

'I can, I truly can!' he cried out and stood up with the batten poised to write his first Words,

In reverie he does not see outside himself;
battered like a religion upon a barren rock,
this exact rock that holds his nakedness,
to sleep whilst standing upon sore soles,
that must work precisely to keep him there...

'Which rock, and of whom do you write? questioned a voice.

'Mere Words!' exploded the Fisherman.

'Mere Words?' asked the whispers.

'Mere Words.' And then trailed away.

Images spun in front of him and he made out a small out-crop of rock twenty-five metres out to Sea.

'There - that rock! You see it? Damn you! You see it there in the Sea. I know that you do.'

The *Majesdad del Color* had now gone, perhaps frightened off by this erratic performance. Suddenly, there was noth-ing there.

'What is happening to me?' sighed the Fisherman.

His attention was suddenly caught by a little something tangled in a corner of his net. The last corner to have come out of the Sea. No proud workman can truly relax at the end of the day until everything has been put back in its rightful place; he walked straight over and began untan-gling this small something.

'A little statue of some sort. A boy,' said the Fisherman

brushing dried seaweed off it. He splashed it about loosening the Sargasso weed and sand that concealed the boy's finer details. He was a foot tall and elegant. The Fisherman held him aloft and was struck for a second by a recollection, so vivid that he let the manikin slip from his grasp. The boy splashed down and looked up from the shallows.

But the boy was singular.

He had a look once seen never forgotten. The very image of the boy he had seen during that horrific vision deep in the eye of the Sea. His throat suddenly felt drier. He couldn't raise any spit now. Shame swept through him as if brought on the breeze. He felt uncomfortable with his own presence - why couldn't he be at peace in this idyllic little bay?

The Fisherman stood the statue up in the sand. He was carved entirely out of wood. The boy had kept a beautiful sharp profile as well as long nimble fingers. The wood was walnut, therefore, extremely resistant to swelling and also determining his dark colour. His carved eyes were far-reaching and furious. They had something to say, a story - his-story. Worn cloth clothes hung loosely from him. The work in his hands, eyes and perfectly woven clothes gave him an air of youthful nobility. His shirt was cream coloured, the sleeves billowed out like a Square Rig's sails from a tight-fitting navy waistcoat. The waistcoat was fastened almost right up, only a single button was missing. The Sea had tarnished the colour of the buttons and worn an emblem down to disjointed lines. His trousers were held up by a woven multicoloured cloth belt. There were holes in his clothes, in his elbows, knees and one across his buttock -

in quite regular places, as if he had been a real boy going about everyday life.

The Fisherman looked down at his own clothes and fingered the patches in the same places. Thinking.

Thoughts.

Just a rubbish collection of piled thoughts.

Sweep them aside.

The old man scanned the horizon to see if there was any change, any likelihood of help at hand.

The film edits flashed "Eleanora" and "Fortuna" at him.

He stood alone.

The bleached space of the beach lay open and wide like an introductory page to a manuscript. With only a few lines he had successfully and surprisingly written himself into the margins. The "barren rock" was but a stone's throw away, the subject of the poem had lain trapped in his net.

The peace was immense. His solitude whole. The blankness in his mind echoed that of the Sea, all of a sudden there was truly nothing, nothing to see. He felt at ease as good friends do when long moments of silence exist between themselves.

This moment had been a long time coming. The Fisherman thought hard. He asked aloud, as if to an audience:

'A lifetime at Sea must surely mean something?'

'Yes, it must. True enough,' came a reply.

'Now sleep.'

'I inherited a Principality from my good father. The changes in time took it from me. It was already a romantic notion when I came of age.'

'So, you are a Prince?' asked the old man in his sleep.

'Everyone can hear, see, smell, touch and imagine his own World. Mine was an image, a nation; I put them together and created an imagination.'

'Truly a magnificent gift!' But why speak as though it had crumbled away so very long ago?'

'It is truly ancient. You have little idea of what I've seen, or how heavy is my satchel of long histories.'

'And where is this heavy satchel?'

'In the net, Fisherman. It is trapped in your net.'

He stirred, rubbed the sweat from his eyebrows with his forearm, rolled on to his side and shakily stood up. The ten paces he took were fragile, almost experimental, as if he had gone back in his lifetime and was making his first steps as a child. His eyes ran over every twist and knot of the net. One colour woven into another - repaired and added to over many years.

There was no satchel.

'I am slipping. The net will outlive me, always to contain moments of a life.'

He held out his left palm and exposed his lifeline religiously before him. Alongside it there also ran the recent groove, cut deep to where pain sings: both lines showing the signs of a hard, long and rewarding life.

'There are two of me sharing this battered and bruised body. One shall be called victory, the other defeat.'

He raised his right hand to his left and opened it out before the Sea. He passed a long and blurry moment star-

ing into his palms where there rose a small but singular cluster of buildings.

'My village,' whispered the Fisherman amazed. 'It is all here, welcoming.'

He saw himself in front of the village, by the Sea, by his recently beached skiff and a net teeming with the rewards of the afternoon's fishing. He had a cigar in his mouth, the hand of an eleven-year-old boy in his own. Together they turned to walk towards the road. The white pueblo smiled down on them, reddened along the rooftops from the sunset over the Sea's horizon. The rising sandy steps circled the main street. All the doors to the houses were ajar; the villagers had mostly come down to assess the catch, some would help prepare the nets.

Then a shadow was cast over the village. The Fisherman turned and looked up at the sky, at the shadow.

'It's a uniformity that steals our ways and our visions,' said a voice.

'Pardon me - uniformity?' he asked.

'There will be only one way eventually. A World where people have broken down distances, where there is nothing to explore and expand themselves. Everything available immediately in a single Word. Or by pushing a button. Language superseded by standardised symbols. This is the World that I see.'

The Fisherman sighed. The sun was already past its strongest point but still ablaze and fiery. It was there to be worshipped like a god; so passionate that it was burning itself out.

The sunset in his palm returned. He saw himself twice - by the Sea as a Fisherman with his son and then seated on a branch high up a tree as a boy. He heard tiny voices, rumours of civilisation. His neighbour holding a cable pointing excitedly towards his television. Stone masons labouring crude reddish stone with tiny precise tapping. A bell of an indescribable size occupied another corner of the square, in front of it was a neatly turned-out gentleman looking at a large drawing decorated with official stamps. The bell was stamped 1542.

He saw a young woman approaching, glowing in the moment. Her dress was cream-coloured with lapped burgundy hems that licked at her knees as she descended with each step towards the shore, the boats and her family.

The boy in the tree suddenly jumped down to the ground as a young girl passed. The girl who was now the woman in the cream-coloured dress headed for the shore. Time was shifting fast in his palms. He saw himself and his son striding over towards the woman.

'Eleanora,' whispered the Fisherman.

He twisted his left hand to reach out for her. He saw his sore hands open in front of him again; burgundy lines of dried blood. He turned towards the palm trees, dropped to his knees, hung his head, extended his palms again and cried aloud a prayer of sorts.

His Words inscribed into the sand rose before him:

In reverie he does not see outside himself;
battered like a religion upon a barren rock

Then passed another voice clearly saying,
'This exact rock that holds his nakedness.'

The old man raised himself, grabbed the batten and violently forced it into the white sand writing:

Until -
He awakens to a Sea caressing his thighs,
surprised by his reaction, he cups his hands
round nothingness and shouts -

The old man swung round and let go of the batten, then
he turned to face the Sea, cupped his hands and shouted,
  'So beautifully bone-white.'

The moment seemed to collapse around him and his Words
flew out into nothingness. He paused, took his gaze across
millions of horizons. Then from out of nowhere they
returned, millions of echoes slapping him in the face:

  Like an angel chiselled out of a block of salt.

The image filled his mind, sealing his emotions fossil-tight
like a fish skeleton in bedrock high up on mountainous
land. Every time a thought came to him it was shouted out.
A lonely performance, a solo act in front of a silent audience whose responses were subtle whisperings, judging,
often well timed, well articulated, sometimes intense, then
softer. Then nothing. A silent response is the worst.

The Fisherman had spent a lifetime developing a special
relationship with his principal audience - the Sea. He had
always and naively thought highly of himself and their relationship, believing to 'feel' the Sea and her caprices. Deep
down, he knew for sure that his feelings were purer than
most - a dedicated lifetime at Sea must amount to a certain knowledge.

He respected his catches and the kill. He knew that the
will to survival was innate in all things that are living. The

work was cruel to create a distance between the Living Sea and himself, however much he dreamt of his final union with the Sea.

He greatly loved things that existed beyond man's ability to kill, to claim and to contaminate. He admired them for simply being unreachable: the sun, the stars, the moon, the wind, the future and the dead.

Horizons lay beyond his reach, in a little twenty-three-foot skiff. But the Sea in its openness had carried grander ships of other continents from such horizons. This was the history of his Island, of himself. Such history was also a source of torment. He often heard echoes that troubled his mind. He was en route like a message in a bottle that had conquered historic time. And now the bottle had finally landed, cracked for the very first time. Echoes, utterances, Words, maps and music had begun to fill the old spaces.

It was now mid-afternoon and the moon was already a faint silvery sphere in the sky. He cooled his body by sitting knee deep in the Sea. It was an effort. The waves didn't want him there. He had to struggle to maintain his position. As the waves retreated he felt the sand below betray him by running away. One powerful sweeping wave dislodged him. He took in saltwater, but quickly coughed it out.

'It is the moon that does this to me,' he thought. 'She who controls the Sea. Her beauty comes only from her position - up there, in the sky. Really she is ill, a patient in a dead vacuum, lifeless and in need of some water - just like me, beyond help, or any salvation.'

He glanced over towards his skiff. The motion of the waves filled, then emptied her of seawater.

'Ah, my skiff still breathes. In and out.'

The packet of cigarettes lay drying in the sun. The line was just as he had left it, coiled up neatly as if prepared to go out again. But the planks of the boat had sprung loose, the upper rising and a supporting thwart; it was utterly unseaworthy. It is a personal blow for a skipper to see his boat in such a condition.

He ran his hands along the boat's capping edge. Wood felt like skin - something alive and breathing to the touch. It was most alive at night when the stem and cut-water divided the Sea. Then there was a shower of sparks, a language that trailed away into the distance, into the confusion of the wake. But the meanings always lingered for longer.

He had carved a petit figurehead, something mystical being half fish and half woman with folded wings at the stem of his skiff, his wife crossed with a Pez Golondrino. He had painted the name of his skiff: Eleanora. She was a muse: everywhere, styled and worn by the motion of the Sea. Her dark-wood reflection could be seen at the stern on the water's surface, pushing the phosphorescent plankton away. **Soon. Come. You.**

This all took place below the silvery hints of the moon. But he still felt the sun on his wet, well-weathered brown skin. A shiver raced right through him and out through his soles. His breathing slowed.

'I am strong and will survive the night.'

He reached for the water-drum and held it up high, tightly to his lips and caught several drops of water. Bracing his arms fully round it, he held it up vertically. A couple of rewarding mouthfuls drained out from a pocket of water trapped around the rim.

The first mouthful was painful and felt abrasive, like he was swallowing a mouthful of sand. His mouth oozed viscous saliva. The second mouthful he held on to, swilled it around his mouth, letting its full flavour and texture seep into his tongue and gums. A hard smile pushed his lips apart. There was a revival of sorts.

He called out defiantly,

'I am strong and will survive the night.'

As if to demonstrate his intention he gripped the drum by the rims and threw it with all his might. Before it hit the ground he turned his back and shouted out over the Sea,

'Not a single quiver of fear!'

There was a thump as the drum hit the sand - a wooden thump like a stick on a timbale.

Turning again the Fisherman realised what he had done.

'Ah, my Prince. Please forgive me.'

He rolled the drum over and seized the manikin by the waist, but dropped him almost immediately. It seemed he saw the familiar silver lights of phosphorescent plankton emanating from the boy's body.

'Oh, forgive me.'

There were no more silver splinters.

'They can only come at night. I have seen them, millions of them. I know when they come - ONLY AT NIGHT.'

His own actions were beginning to puzzle him. He put his left palm down against the heat of the sand. The heat increased in the wound. He twisted on his palm and sunk down into the sand, cross-legged. The boy he positioned squarely in front of him. The Sea chased up and lapped both pairs of feet.

'You are a work of art my friend. Beautifully crafted,' admired the Fisherman.

He looked at the boy's walnut-coloured eyes and their fine detail. He thought that once they might have been painted, maybe blue-black like his once were.

Time passed.

The boy spoke in a soft but authoritative voice, 'you said that you would sit me upon that rock. That seems like a good idea. So get up and sit me upon History's Rock and we'll start again, as if we had never known one another, never met. What do you say?'

'OK, but we have never met.'

'We have. Over many years our paths have crossed. I have accompanied you at Sea, looked out for your wellbeing. I approached you once, but that was bad timing on my part. You weren't the man you now are.'

The old man stared hard at the manikin. He recalled the vision of the boy entering the bar and the spit hurtling from between his lips. He looked away ashamed.

'You have now a greater peace. But that's enough of this white space. Let's say that you take me over to that rock. It is but a stone's throw away.'

'I must conserve my energy, last out the night,' said the old man.

'I can give you my Word that this will be so.'

The old man shakily stood up and gauged the distance. The rock was barely twenty-five metres away. If his skiff had been half-seaworthy he would have pushed it out and hand-paddled it over.

He bent over to pick up the boy but couldn't raise him from the sand.

He shook his head, bracing his legs to try and lift the boy a second time.

'I am still master of my own strength,' he declared. Bending slightly at the knees and shoulders he turned and stepped triumphantly into the Sea with the boy held closely to his chest.

'My heart is strong,' claimed the old man. 'I can hear the boom-boom that echoes in my ears when I dream, when my body is pressed against the keel. This is the instrument that plays throughout those long nights.'

He waded further out until a light wave rose above his knee showering him with fragmented Words - the poetry of a mildly troubled mind:

Wash, wash
Seamless Sea
Spilling over
History's soils
Push, pull
Come in me
A language
Secret's syllables
Must I wait
Must I starve
So far
From sight
Seek and see
Words dissolved
Dishonouring me

'The Sea is a tangled tissue of sensitive nerves like my mind,' thought the Fisherman, 'but all this makes no sense to me. These whispers and murmurs come from a depth that my lines have never reached.'

He felt the weight of the boy in his arms, but his legs were moving weightlessly through the Sea. His body was still finely tuned; well fed over many years by the Sea's energy, enriched by the sun. The tautness of his muscles and the texture of his skin denied his regal age. Only his eyes were old. The strain of a long life hung across them like worn velvet curtains across a bright window with a wide-reaching view. They soaked up the brilliance that once would have mirrored off them like the wet film on freshly opened mother of pearl. They were still the colour of mother of pearl, but old, as those set in antique furniture with a ring of brown at the edges.

The weight became overbearing and spots swam before his eyes. They were popping in front of him, large and small. He tried to eliminate them by straining his eyes open wide.

The Pinks and Purples of this World popped and the blackness returned.

Into the Sea plunged the old man with the boy.

Somehow, he had felt a rock ledge and pulled himself upwards. He did so with tremendous force, breaking through the surface panting for air. His chest and underarms were badly cut by barnacles. The cuts were neat, deep and clean as if done by a doctor's scalpel; but there was no doctor at hand to get his strength back up, to give him food and water. He sat exhausted with his elbows upon his knees, his heavy head wilting into his sore stinging palms. A thickset silver chain hung forward from his neck to below his palms. He looked like a destitute prisoner handcuffed at the wrists.

The boy was lost. His own solitude and recklessness inflamed him.

'Fool! You fool!' he shouted out.

He heard the waves calling:

History

His – to - ry

Then he remembered the brilliance of his underwater vision and the deliverance from pain. His movements through the water had been slow but soothing, enveloping him in guiding tentacles that pushed the ochre heat of the sun way into the background. Everything seemed effortless.

He was no longer hunting, killing, employing trickery; there was no duty to fetch life from the Sea. Suddenly he was alive with it and sharing its qualities. He felt unique. The respectful fear had disappeared - the one that man harbours, always, with the knowledge that his strength is secondary, his life beyond his ultimate control. There was no need for the ritual asking for protection - he was supported from all angles by the Sea's soothing mass.

He vaguely remembered walking along a soft bed, his feet sinking in. The boy was with him. Reflected light came from above the surface. The boy was always slightly in front. He was reading to the Fisherman - not from a book but from scorings made in the seabed. As each Word was read out it grew fainter as they passed over it, then it vanished altogether. The boy seemed to have done this before. Perhaps many times before. Still, his heart was filled by what he read aloud,

Where is the end of them, the Fisherman sailing
Into the wind's tail, where the fog cowers?
We cannot think of a time that is oceanless
Or of an ocean not littered with wastage
Or of a future that is not liable
Like the past, to have no destination. *9

'I don't understand. How can a past have no future?'

The Fisherman stopped, the boy passed through him and came about to face him.

'All life originated from the Sea,' he said, 'from water. We always equate life with time, so without the ocean there never was any time, never any life, and this is beyond our imagination. We can also speak of a past that never had any viable future - this has happened to many: this unfortunate life returns to the Sea, abandoned in a vastness of future hopes.'

The Fisherman thought aloud,

'All that littering, wastage, life's openness to creation, but never having anywhere to settle, or to rest. But...'

The boy walked forwards into the Fisherman and forced him several steps back. The boy began his reading afresh,

For our own past is covered by the currents of action,
But the torment of others remains an experience
Unqualified, unworn by subsequent attrition.
People change, and smile: but the agony abides.
Time the destroyer is time the preserver,
Like the river with its cargo of dead Negroes, cows and
chicken coops,
The bitter apple and the bite in the apple.
And the ragged rock in the restless waters,

Waves wash over it, fogs conceal it;
On a halcyon day it is merely a monument,
In a navigable weather it is always a seamark
To lay a course by: but in the sombre season
Or the sudden fury, is what it always was.   *10

The Fisherman dropped to his knees and frantically tried to prevent the Words from vanishing. The boy stood up. The Fisherman followed angrily,
    'Damn you! I simply do not understand. I cannot be what you wish of me.'
    'We seek nothing,' said the boy nonchalantly.
    'We?' asked the old man.
    A million voices shouting 'YES, WE' flew back at him.

The old man reached through the water. His fingers found a ledge on the bedrock and he used it to heave himself up.
    He surfaced very alone.
    The restless waves were lapping against the rock where he now sat. The Fisherman chose not to hear them. The Pinks and Purples of this World blotted out this picture of Paradise, that painless World. Whatever had happened to him was now over.

The rock began to dig into the Fisherman's buttocks and the soles of his feet. Yet he preferred not to move. The pain had returned, along with a question he repeated,

'Why me - porque yo?'

His hair had dried rough in the wind. It bushed in thick curls that covered his fingers as he pushed it back from his forehead. His pose resonated with the hero suffering isolated tragedy.

Battered.
Beaten.
Bruised.
And Torn.

He now wore all these telling masks as the sun set over the Sea. He cried and cried in the weak presence of the stars.

Eleanora, his son, his Pueblo and the church bells rang and rang in his ears:

'We are all waiting for you here.'
'Come back soon.'
'Please come to me.'

The Fisherman dried his eyes unashamedly. There was no one to see him: a victim without a witness.

'I will sit this night out peacefully,' figured the Fisherman. 'Bring myself into it as if I was sailing my skiff home with the *vientos alisios* *11. There will be no sleep this night as eternal sleep is coming... At least I have company in the stars; beyond man's reach, beyond my suffering.'

The sun had partially slipped into the Sea. Rumours ran like a panicked tribe throughout the kingdom of the

Majesdad del Azul Salvaje. The sun was setting; those that come out at night were stirring, hungry, whilst those that used the night to rest, to hide, began to retreat to greater depths.

Now the waves made no splashes. The sun's head was cracked and bleeding. It must die too. And very soon.

Every poem takes something out of its creator.

The stage scenery changed rapidly - the stars were painted white then plunged into silver glitter before the paint had time to dry. The moon appeared at the flick of a switch. The spotlight fell onto the Fisherman from high up in the heavens. Some of the channelled light spilled and scattered energy across the sleepless Sea.

'Do you rest now?' the Fisherman asked. 'At times I think you are dreaming. At times there is the movement of millions'.

He paused, then whispered,

'I must say a prayer.'

He gazed a little out to Sea. Facing him were the lines of the boy's poem. They were very bright and white. His pulse raced, the Words bouncing round his body, pumped by the pounding rhythm of his heart.

But the torment of others remains an experience

He picked out certain Words and phrases and recalled the crossing to the rock. He found himself mumbling,

People change,
the river...
cargo of dead Negroes,

And the ragged rock in the restless waters,
Waves wash over it,
conceal it;
it is merely a monument,
seamark
sombre season.
is what it always was.

He looked away towards the shore and there he saw the
Words to his own poem bright below the stars:

In reverie he does not see outside himself;
battered like a religion upon a barren rock,
this exact rock that holds his nakedness,
to sleep whilst standing upon soles,
that work precisely to keep him there...

His scorings were very prominent. But they were not the
only etchings visible. The beach was littered with Words,
broken phrases, fragmented texts and tales of other
Worlds. He blinked and read more Words and phrases:

Notions of evolution,
rigging and the aerial,

Home, speechless we came,
desert, when do I return?
Starved ankles,

my Island drifts aimlessly like a turtle's back half out of the
Sea

Vinieron aquel día muchas canoas a regatear algodón hilado y hamacas de red que son donde ellos duermen.

flotsam, jetsam -
keep stars, heavens dangerous doors,
where we are not permitted to enter

Seal mouth, speak
No more

Pescaron con redes y hallaron un pez que parecía puerco, cubierto todo de concha, lo único blando eran sus ojos y su cola.

This is the order

LISTEN, in his right hand
was as the sun shineth in his strength.

Seven stars

For we wrestle not against flesh and blood, but against principalities, against powers, against the rulers of the darkness of this world, against....

The Fisherman blinked his eyes again and read:

Seal mouth, speak
No more

Where had all these other personalities come from? They had trespassed into his poem. But surely he wasn't the first person to have inhabited this space? He felt helpless. His last moments would be echoes of countless other troubled minds. Hunger gnawed him deep.

'I am who I am,' he stated matter-of-factly, 'and that is a strong old Fisherman. I do not wish to be another disembodied voice blowing from the past without a place of rest, without a destination. I won't join the rotting hulls...'

The Fisherman bent forwards and whilst squatting he dipped his hands into the Sea. The phosphorescent plankton randomly raced in a thousand-thousand directions. His eyes danced with them until long after their energies had been dispersed.

'They have always ran wild in these Seas'.

He had never ceased to be amazed by them. Like an amazed boy he would kneel over the bows, running his fingers and forearms through the Sea and marvelling at the silver electrical effect.

A warm night-breeze chased low over the Sea. The smell of salt was stronger. It made his skin and hair sticky to the touch. Even his breath tasted saltier, as if he was crystallising from the inside out.

He tapped his chest and sighed, a thoughtful sigh as memories of days gone by. The Fisherman felt at ease in his own company. His father had always said:

'Isolation has much in its favour. One learns to search inwardly and gain self-respect, independent from the opinions of others.'

The years at Sea had sealed his father's Words, as if they were gospel. His father had spent much time alone as a

Fisherman and as a radical - the other villagers kept their exchanges with him short, but courteous. But he used to debate with visitors whilst he sat on the sand repairing his nets. Raised voices would often be heard.

His father had once said to him,

'Keep away from the bible. It has always been a pretext for such an insatiable greed. In his Personal Narrative, Alexander Von Humboldt did more for our America than any European conqueror or ambassador. He demonstrated the need for Science, progress and understanding, respect and consideration for Nature.'

Then he would reach under the bows for his book wrapped in plastic - his 'Bible'. He would pull it out, exclaim 'Oh yes', unwrap it and then leaf through the salty and stuck pages and read aloud; his audience - one inspired Fisherman's boy and the Sea. He took deep breaths before starting and would often gaze at his son from over the top of the pages.

'Listen to this son, this is how Humboldt describes our World. "Every one thing exists for the sake of all things and all for the sake of one; for the one is of course the all as well. Nature, despite her seeming diversity, is always a unity, a whole...a relationship to the rest of the system." *12

'There are always such tensions,' he said once, 'such struggles, the to-ing and fro-ing is never greater than when one is afloat on the Sea. You hear voices don't you son? Pause and listen.'

The Fisherman heard himself answering,

'No father I don't. Please, what are they telling you?'

It was many years before he did.

His father's voice grew stronger again in his memory. He

was reading,

"It was as if we heard distant voices echoing across the ocean, magically carrying us from one hemisphere to another." *13

The Fisherman remained leaning forwards with his hands dipped into the Sea, lost in time and contemplation. The phosphorescent plankton left marks of their journeys. The contours of the rock below were barely visible. They looked like a dark map, like a cruel confession in black and royal blue ink. This truly was the ragged rock in the restless waters. He longed for dawn to change the mood. To escape from History Rock.

The old man gazed at the North Star. Even with a seaworthy boat he wouldn't ever make it home now. He had been defeated well before the storm attacked and discarded him upon this surreptitiously crowded shoreline.

That long terrible fight with the fish! How he had to kill it at all costs, to show the others that he was more than an old man shadowed by a cloud of bad luck... And so many weeks at Sea and hardly a single fish taken. And if the fish had only surrendered days earlier... Now they both had to die, weakened beyond recuperation, both out of their depths. The Fisherman realised that he was too weary to return. Home was now a place in his mind.

'The uniformity,' he murmured staring into the sky as he made out the darkness approaching. He shivered and the hunger cramped his stomach. He coughed painfully. Bile tastes far worse than saltwater. He spat it out. No phosphorescent lights appeared.

He thought again of conversations with his father.

'Imagine, son, being here, forever in the middle, when suddenly the horizon fills with a threat. It doesn't appear so very far away then, and this is no longer such a solitary place. The horizon brought them here; it all happened so very quickly that now it is mostly forgotten. But they're coming again, only slower this time, much bigger, louder and with more of a strategy. I'm not the first person to say that history's wheel is turning against us once again; repeating itself.'

The Fisherman felt a part of the whole story on the Sea. The Sea brought the World to him, told him of capital cities, continents and cultures. These voyages were as much internal as physical. He covered great distances from the inside, out. He would stand facing out to Sea and upright in front of the small mast, his legs tightly together and his arms held rigidly outright like a statue of Christ being transported by Sea from the Old World and to be placed high in the New.

He knew that he was vulnerable and that the Sea was a voice for lost souls, but distrust was never a part of their relationship. The horizon was filled with events in the making as well as in the past. They came unannounced.

One day as he stood Christ-like, the horizon blurred and the sky appeared as a frosty mirror. Eddies swirled, densely forested peaks rose through the disturbance and pierced the mirror's back. Heavy clean clouds scattered rain upon the steep emerging slopes. He had been surprised to hear voices. He saw a city - and one with no bell towers. An architectural wonder, the stones appeared irregularly placed, trapezoid blocks. A bass hum emanated from inside the most central buildings - a possible religious service. He could hear children's voices, not in there, but coming from behind the city, over towards the valley.

There was a majestic river in the valley. It spoke an ono-matopoetic language. The people could speak it also, as could the mountains. The river was coming from far away, from very high up, from a place frequented only by ice flow-ers and the wildest, toughest and most elusive animals. Such mysterious animals inspired these people's imagina-tions - he could see wild cats, great birds with powerful wingspans and unknown terrifying beasts carved into the façades and stone steps.

He saw what looked like a map detailing the surrounding mountaintops visible from this sacred city. It also was carved out of stone and raised upon a ceremonial plinth.

Maps, Maps... To know where one is, to plan where one must go in relation to where one has been. We become richer for having made the journey, every step defines the place where one begins:

> We shall not cease from exploration
> And the end of all our exploring
> Will be to arrive where we started
> And know the place for the first time.   *14

The Fisherman indeed knew this city, this sacred place. It was the true beginnings of America. These stones were monumental, the bones of hard labour, of civilisation and they spoke. He knelt overwhelmed on the shore of his con-tinent. All life came from the Sea. He cupped his hands and scooped up some sandy soil. The tragedy and power of the earth ran through his fingers. The Fisherman could smell wonderful scents of flowers, fruits, rivers, woodlands and grasslands. It was all so new to him, but the experience was short-lived. There was a terrific eruption - a separation of history. There were voices everywhere scrambling in the dark clouds encircling the mountaintops. Then they were heard no more. The Fisherman returned to the Sea.

The waves rose silvery up the rock filling the pools and cracks with life and movement, like watching starved lungs filling with fresh oxygen. The Fisherman shakily scrambled towards the top of the rock. It was no bigger than a large roof terrace. The sides were fairly steep, cut jagged like an evil grin from a cruel mouth. At the top the Fisherman found a welcoming surprise. There was a small flattened area of wind and storm polished rock, just bigger than a man, a little space of comfort, a place of softness away from the continual restlessness of the Sea; something similar to home.

He leant forward towards the Sea with his arms stretched o - u - t -

Wash. Pause.
Ripple. Wash.
Sea. Saw.
Word. Hear.
Rise. Fall.
Run. Free.

The stars and moon shimmered across the Sea's surface randomly like an inspired painter placing his first rapid brush stokes across a clean canvas. The poems from the Seabed had long since disappeared, only their subtleties of meaning roamed undefined in the Fisherman's mind. He couldn't forget them. The poem had performed in public and he had been the only one there to appreciate it. He claimed the poem for himself, he felt the happier for it; he would leave this World with something close to his heart.

Emotion.
Freedom.
Run.

But there was always the line, taught and unforgiving – a Sea anchor that refused to surface, wedged in the heart of a life that didn't wish to give it up. So they must fight. Struggle. Suffer. Man and Fish.

He remembered shouting at the fish deep below,

'Why do you kill us both? There is no sense in this. I love you and you must give up now - let yourself go!'

There were echoes all around him:

I said to my soul, be still and wait without hope

The Fisherman drooped, his limbs hung loosely from his tired frame. His eyes stared at the polished, flattened rock bed. He could just make out the shell of a crustacean, the occupant long since gone from History Rock. He conceded to the notion of dying. The light breeze - *la brisa de la noche* - passed through his old bones.

'God, I am so tired. So very ill. I just can't...'

Tears welled up in the Fisherman's eyes. The mother of pearls moistened and this fetched the shine out of them once again. Tears encased in silver moonlight ran from the corner of his eyes, plummeted to the rock. The silver changed to red. One, two, three, thirty-three teardrops flashed below at his feet.

His eyes began to fill with the reddish flickerings. Suddenly there was light - Hope. He wiped his eyes dry with his sore hands and exclaimed jubilantly,

'¡Cocuyos!'

And indeed they were lighting up the rock surface like fire torches might have done in the darkened passageways of the Mayan temples.

'How bizarre that they are here on this barren rock. There are no branches or leaves or grass. Cocuyos do not live on rocks out at Sea!'

Like emergency flares, they were lost too.

The Fisherman remembered how Eleanora adored these simple phosphorescent insects. She would collect them from the nearby forests, place them in a gourd pierced with tiny, eccentrically patterned holes and from in front of the doorway she would stand with her back to the night and say,

'Our son sleeps now. Let's go for a walk by Cocuyos light.'

She would shake the gourd to excite the little Cocuyos who reacted by flickering and burning red, enveloping her in the red hue of her tiny friends who burnt themselves out for her. They had always done this for her. The Fisherman in an instant saw the magic of the woman he had married - she had always remained so.

He had first noticed her as a girl in this strongest of natural lights. Some years later she had shown him the contents of her gourd and shaken it. Both their faces had glowed in the illuminant disks of their bodies. The years seemed to freeze in memory. It was this intense colourful energy that had sparked his desire for her. She was exu-

berant. Her wide-eyed look so expressive and mildly wild.
The Cocuyos lights had given her all away, lighting her
blooming youth under the shadow of the whispering palm
leaves. A path had lit up for him. The calling of her colours
had drawn him closer to her body. Intrigued and fascinat-
ed by the magic of the moment, by her breath settling
upon him, he had reached out further, tasted her lips and
the hot breath where all her spoken Words must pass.
There he had lingered unsure of what might have been said
had he not been so close as to bar their passage. Suddenly
it was all Thoughts and Interpretations. Between two people.

So many ways to say.
Something.
Like.
Love.

He'd found her lips soft like the underside of rose petals.
They opened and closed gently as his own rubbed smooth-
ly over hers. Playfully to begin with, then seriously. There
was no refusal. Their families remained somewhere behind
them, unaware, asleep. To he and Eleanora the World was
being changed.

From out of the Sea's dark body emerged a misty blan-
ket. It was warm and carried a fine sheen of silvery dew. It
filtered across them and to every blade of Sea grass, every
leaf and stirring flower bud. A snail's back glistened under
the dew, touched by nature's fingers. Leaves no longer rustled and cracked as they did in the sun. The lovers too
were clothed in this silvery spray. The Sea pulsed. Told
them not to talk. Merely to be. Free. Entwined, and
unaware of time so that minutes would wash away, filter

through the grains of sand. Through one another.

And the dew brought with it a coolness that had stiffened their bodies. Both wine-red under the burning of the Cocuyos. The Fisherman remembered easing his back against the knotted trunk of his most revered *Palma Real*.

He had brought her towards him. Her legs straddled over his own and she had moved higher up to meet him. Her hair hung low, blanketing out their bashful unbelieving stares. And those trembling whites of their eyes. Her thick twisting curls covered them both from any shame or guilt.

Freedom.

The trembling of such freedom.

To move.

To move through this unfathomable Sea where Boy held onto Girl. Woman onto Man. She'd felt his new fear tighten the softness of his lips. She took his fear, warmed it in her touch, in her motions. Her breasts found his mouth. The hollowness eager and alive. She'd felt herself warming within. Excited, he had shivered briefly into the coolness of the night as if shedding any final inhibitions. She too shivered, more lightly than he. Her motions had left wetness across his stomach. It kissed the dew's sheen and smelt of jungles after a storm.

The Sea's whisperings rose, came before her as if coming from him. She'd breathed in deeply and the rumours chased within her. Out of her. She closed her soft eyes. Gently the silvery breaths warmed them both. They had passed all uncertainties.

She tasted him there, all before him, his skin - the salt came from him, from his blood. From the Sea. His taste lingered for an eternity on the tip of her tongue.

Balanced.

Like. This.

He would, somehow, forever be there.

Forever.

The outside World receded and seemed unrecoverable. Together they were swimming. No gravity or loose ground to deceive them. To send them bouncing right back. He'd placed his supple yet line-toughened hands upon her waist. Then down and round her buttocks. Softly. So. Slowly. He beckoned her down. Their lips demanded kiss upon kiss. No pauses. No denials. No distinctions. Not now.

They'd held their breaths tightly and sunk slowly. And it was then that she'd felt him firm below her. The smoothness of his erection had teased her. Brought her closer, then away.

The Fisherman remembered that very first abundance of joy; the moving and pushing deeper, occasionally tugging at her nipples with his mouth, biting, nearly too hard, at times. The dreaming. The reality. The cementing of their love. Together and luminous in the Cocuyos light they'd remained in an intense red, that diminished as the night receded, the dream spent and the orange rose above the million shades of uniform blueness.

The fishermen had begun preparing their lines.

Their nets.

Their trickery.

And. Say it.

Morning had broken.

As the Sea was his secret World, this was hers - a place where the Fisherman was merely an intimate guest. And in her World her magic translated the austere cold blue seamless Sea into many shades of red, sunsets and dreams, the burning red oils of precious perfumes and scents, the minerals in rich red wine, the place where the blood of the nation is originated - la sangre del Pueblo tiene rico perfume.

As the Fisherman's wife, the openness and changeability of the Sea worried her; he was far too often a mere dot upon the horizon. Then one last wink of the eye - blink - and he would be gone - gone to another who carried him dangerously further and further away.

He had 'disappeared' before. For three long days. The villagers had said many prayers. Each morning carried a different diminishing hope with those echoes of inevitability expressing little, 'one never knows'.

He returned just before dawn on the fourth day. The village was soundly sleeping. The salty air carried the smell of rising bread from the baker's ovens. He carefully opened the door to his house, crept in and looked around him as he always did after returning from long fishing trips. He found a folded rough cream envelope propped up against a wineglass on the drawer. It was marked:

The Fisherman's Wife - A Letter.

It read:

We grew up together in a white-washed pueblo.
I was dressed to my parents' tastes.
Together our youths were spent combing beaches.
Our lands were locked, fearing greater things.
We knew no fear when looking towards horizons!
Futures were other Worlds.
Two small people, outside of time.

Far too young, I married you. My innocence a
                                    whited torch.
By night, flickering cocuyos illuminated the
                              way. Playing with red,
My secrets were exposed, beneath my lowered
                                              head.
They flickered in their calling, over and over
                                              again.
Suddenly, my life was sealed.
I turned away from the sea whilst you were
                                      out there,
And faced the village walls.

My naive existence couldn't keep you.
All I wanted was for your red shadows to
                              mingle with mine.
And never to depart, never, never, never again.
From this very shore, I now look out to sea,
                        asking of myself,
'What should I be seeking in such a lonely
                              horizon?'

That was after you last put out to sea,
Alone, in the rough after-waters of your father.
Young and free 'till old: Tradition thus is deep
And you have been gone for such time now;
Each evening me him a prayer with salty
                                    tongues of silence.

That last day I saw you dragging your skiff over
                            the white sands;
One, two, three paces, then you jumped in, then
                            were carried away
The church bells rg earlier this season over
                            the town.
The wind sang solemn notes, too slow to whistle
                            along with
The cowslips no longer flicker with the deep red
                            intensity we both knew.
Why, just over there, across our beach, nature
                    has become lazy upon
                        the throne.
It is advancing thickly, and it tricks me. Does
                    not treat me the same way.

Anyway, if you are marooned somewhere beyond
                        that horizon,
Write me soon and, with a little note,
I will be there too.

Please reply to my words, calling out to You.

Eleanora — the fisherman's wife.

The poem swelled within the Fisherman. Eleanora reached out to him with every syllable. Her images rich, her tone of humble emotion and delicate. Every line was a single message, a completed chapter, a telegraph wired to him.

Her poem was a call, calling the Fisherman back from the restlessness of the Sea, back from that place where there was no-return, where the realisation that he may not be coming back was a very strong one. Feeling this possibility, she decided to call out to the secret place that only she and the Fisherman knew of - a place of union exposed in a magical reddish hue of the Cocuyos disks,

Write me soon and, in a moment,
I will be there too.
Please reply to my words...

Reply, reply, reply...

On the beach the Fisherman could just make out the shadowy profile of his skiff. Perhaps he could also see the faint markings Eleanora.

'She is with me. She is calling out to me. She has come with the Cocuyos. How else would they have made it here?' He stood silent on the rock for a moment as if waiting for a reply.

'Thank God. I will not be another lost soul, blowing across a boundless Sea. Put me to rest with beautiful thoughts such as these.'

The phosphorescent insects flickered and the red hue intensified. The breeze blew stronger, this excited them, but the Sea stayed unaffected by this increase. A Sea brume drifted in on the trade wind Southwest - the wind that could have filled his sails and gently pushed him homeward. The brume was whispery thin, opaque; it had the changeable shape of a ghostly crowd walking toward him. The temperature dropped as the brume scaled and engulfed the sides of the rock. The Cocuyos shone intermittently, their red growing fainter as the mist thickened.

The Fisherman's mood deepened.

Voices, bass rumbles and cries echoed from every direction. There was a crowd passing over the rock. He felt like he was being swallowed. In fear he twisted backwards and fell. He looked up to see a face emerging out of the mist.

It was an old man's face, full of sorrow, yet so strong, timeless. The old man was walking and didn't appear to notice him. He looked severe like some ancient seer in deep and moody contemplation.

The voices rose and faded, came and went like a terrible dream being screened in the dark of his imagination. A single voice was saying,

the fisherman's boat is broken on the first white inland hills,
his tangled nets in a lonely tree,
the trapped fish still confused.
After this breach of the sea's balanced

treaty, how will new maps be drafted?
Who will suggest a new tentative frontier?
How will the sky dawn now? *15

There was a pause and a million voices shouted in concert,
How will the sky dawn now?

Silence   ————————————

The mist continued to drift over the rock and the Fisherman. It thinned by the second. He was numbed to the bone, struck white with horror. The ghost of the seer now trailed behind the crowd. Nobody seemed to notice him, or appear concerned. Then he saw his father, lost-at-Sea years ago, by the seer's side, looking down at his son. He began to read to him as when they were together the two of them in the skiff. He read clearly, his Words cutting through the crowd,

For on this ground
trampled with the bull's swathe of whips
where the slave at the crossroads was a red anthill
eaten by moonbeams, by the holy ghosts
of his wounds

the Word becomes
again a god and walks among us;
look, here are his rags,
here is his crutch and his satchel
of dreams; here is his hoe and his rude implements

on this ground
on this broken ground.   *16

'Father,' mumbled the Fisherman.

The mist now so faint that it was a silvery whisper in the diminishing night.

The last thing he remembered seeing was the seer clutching a stick and a satchel loosely slung over his shoulder with a collection of loose tools in his right hand. He had walked slowly. He kept walking out to Sea. And then He was gone.

The night dimmed to a lugubrious greyness. The Fisherman shivered and extended himself upon the flat rock, brushing the crustacean shell aside. The rock wasn't warm and grainy like the wood of his skiff. He joined his two sore palms together, as if held in prayer, and tucked them under his cheek. The Cocuyos encircled him as he was carried off in warm sleep.

"And in a moment, I will be there too."

Pain
Sleep
Warmth
Dream
Wake -

The revolution completed, the Fisherman woke with a coppery taste in his mouth. The sun's position read early morning. The moon was still a visible white in the pale blue. His body felt stiff but not cold. His mind for an extended moment was blank. He wished to keep it that way; disengaged from the past, from the disembodied voices, from his predicament. The taste in his mouth was vile. He wanted to retch and then rinse his mouth out, but he had nothing on his stomach and nothing to drink. His tongue was puffy and swollen. When he finally sat up on his elbows, dizziness rushed to his head. He had to close his eyes and wait. He opened them again to note the advancement made overnight by the black clouds from the north.

'Uniformity. A terrible uniformity sweeping over this

World. I once inherited a principality. The changes of time took it from me. Sit me upon History's Rock. How heavy is my satchel...'

The conversations with the boy manikin were circling with his blood, pumped fresh to his mind. Shakily the Fisherman stood up. A sudden splash drew him to a rock-pool where a Pez Golondrino was trapped. His shadow passing over the pool had startled it. He cupped his hands, pushed them into the water to the elbows. He quickly cornered the fish and moved his hands towards it. The flying fish leapt out of the pool, hit the Fisherman's chest and landed at the foot of a stumpy natural column. It seemed like it had been added after the rest of the rock.

He rapped the fish on the head until its eyes blooded and quickly began to chew. It was painful opening his mouth to take a bite. He sat cross-legged by the stone column and ate wholeheartedly. From there he noticed a worn canvas satchel, cream coloured, placed at the other side of the column, and slightly concealed.

'How heavy is my satchel,' he heard the boy say again.

He remembered the mist, the crowd that noisily filed through him, the face of the seer, his father reading:

the Word becomes
again a god and walks among us;
look, here are his rags,
here is his crutch and his satchel
Of dreams

The Fisherman recalled everything now:

'Here is his hoe and his rude implements/on this ground/on this broken ground.'

Things were becoming clearer. The Fisherman was beginning to feel less fear, his pain was easing and his sense of interpretation was all the more astute.

'The seer had been carrying this very bag. Then that perhaps had truly been my father!'

His dream of the Lost City drifted through his mind. The stone column on History Rock was like the plinth that bore the stone map. Out of the satchel had fallen a pile of tools; in his reading, his father had mentioned 'his rude implements'.

The Fisherman handled them individually. There were seven tools, each one well used. A hammer, several chisels and pointed scoring instruments, a ruler-straightedge and a stone polishing tool. They were tools for cutting and working stone. The hammer and chisels had worn handles, polished and smooth where many hands had held them before. Now they were on loan, they didn't belong to him, perhaps to the old seer who had come again to walk among them as a god.

He remembered that the crowd had ignored him. They didn't understand him.

'Look', the poem had instructed us, 'here are his rags'.

In this respect, he was like Jesus - a humble prophet jeered at by the multitude. There was a distance, a respected difference, and this difference was the root to his power. The Fisherman balanced the hammer across his left palm. His mind was explosive - a mine field. Every step a BANG!

BANG: Belonging
BANG: Word
BANG: Voices
BANG: Kingdoms
BANG: Destinations
BANG: Names
BANG: Islands
BANG: Tradition
BANG: Love
BANG: Injustice
BANG: Revolution
BANG: Peace
BANG: Paths of Ancestors
BANG: Setting suns.

The hammer toppled over and the metal chinked against the chisel lying on the rock. He was inspired - and this inspiration far exceeded his suffering. He knew that he would be free soon. And that this freedom would come announced, relinquishing him of responsibility and guiding him, like a gull steering them across the Sea under the shadow of his outstretched wings. The Fisherman was no longer in control, he waited only for the gull to turn his head towards him, quiver his feathers for flight and then they both would be gone.

Now he could face the hooded hordes of the deserted tombs, scavengers with little history seeking out the bones of past tongues to claim as their own.

The Fisherman remembered his Words. His poem,

In reverie he does not see outside himself;
battered like a religion upon a barren rock

He felt more Words rising within him.

The Sea was warm.

The sun broke as fragments of silver upon the surface. He eased himself down from the rock-ledge, then pushed forwards until he was afloat, weightless, swimming to shore like he was a boy again with Eleanora swimming by his side.

The skiff's upper timbers were dry, parched, it seemed as if the wood had already lost some of its colour. It no longer had the oily essence of life, the secret perfume; it was dead to the touch. The Fisherman ran his fingers along the capping and thwart. The dryness brought on a great sadness.

He stood back from it and a wave pushed it towards him again. The Word "Fortuna" caught his eye. Then the wave drew the skiff backwards. He read its name "Eleanora".

It was the film that he had woken up to on his first morning, now it all seemed a lifetime ago, not yesterday. And that it hadn't been him lying there at all in such an abandoned condition. The scene was only a trick. Really he was watching an old reel of film jerking along in front of a dusty projector bulb.

He looked around the beach. There was his outstretched net, patched and repaired so diligently over many years. There was his poem.

With the baton he began to score into the sand once again:

    Nature treats him as an equal;
    equally merciless,
    the Sea, colder in rising,
    seems blacker than blue somehow,
    breaking gently his bare bones,
    against the rocks where,
    marooned, He dreams in prayers;
    His moods succumb to the Muse.

He turned to face the Sea; holding the baton aloft he whispered upon the openness as before,
   'Not a single quiver of fear.'
   The sun was up across its highest point. Beads of sweat found their way into his eyes. The salt stung them considerably. He was past caring. He sat cross-legged upon the sand and shut the horizon and the sun out. The poem was swelling within him; it was now a part of him, something that contained his character and was going to still be there after he had left the World. The brilliant sand preserved the scorings like it was performing a duty of immortality.
   Seated upon the sand he stepped shakily through the minefield of his imagination.

   BANG: Tempo.

Rhythm.
   Sound...
   On this unknown shore a mostly-naked man with smoke billowing from his mouth stood enveloped in its mist and dancing in it, dancing hard to wood and stretched skin. Behind him there were thirty, forty, fifty maybe sixty fat palms beating the skins. The jungle resonated, it shook

with the force and intent. The knife-like leaves of the *Palmas Reales* shivered as if warning strangers of a mighty presence hiding behind this unruly curtain.

The Captain did not understand this display. He viewed it from the top deck, wary of what he saw and heard as well as being drawn towards it: the contradiction that comprises fear. He ordered a steady course.

There were rumours spreading fast amongst the hungry crew,

'But that was Gold around their necks, was it not?'

'Oro, si, mucho oro.'

This was radical: the beat, the feat, the darkness and the strangeness of a new wilderness - Nature, a Paradise Lost: a second innocence, savage and waiting to be tamed and given the Word. The seer emerged from the centre of the group, chanting a rhythm in a language that reflected older Worlds. His face was painted brightly over the dark. His eyes burst through and contained it all. Behind him danced the crowd, echoing his Words. He was dressed in his rags, but he held the crowd with his power: the Word, a god, the Word becomes/again a god and dances for our very souls.

The seer bent forwards with his palms open and fingers flickering. Provocation. His feet drummed the beach, fast and complex. He held his breath. Everything came to a standstill. Somewhere within the jungle an ancient call rang out. It echoed. The crowd reached for the sky, heads tilted upwards as they replied. The seer spun round on the spot: so many revolutions, so many twirling faces, so much beauty, so many songs...

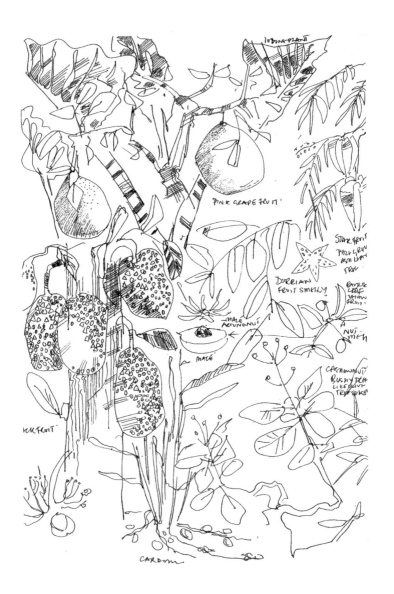

IODINE PLANT

PINK GRAPE FRUIT

STAR FRUIT
PINK GROW
ASH LEAF
TREE

DURRIAN
FRUIT SMELLY

SMALL
LEAF
YELLOW
FRUIT

MALE
ARUNDNUI

A
NUT-
MEG

MALE

CASHEWNUT
BUSHY PEA
LIKE LEAVE
TREE SHRUB

JAK FRUIT

CARDOM

In Havana, the double bass sits on its spike, the fat godfather of Jazz, fingering the vibrating grain of experience. Its melody bridged the calls and responses between Old and New Worlds. We know that in spite of all our hopes, things might not work out for the best: this is how we feel our Jazz. For now though, it's pure fun. Big smiles, white teeth, smoke, black suits, '50s cars with glinting teeth and chrome, rum, ice, cool glasses and gorgeous girls. The rum goes down in the sun; the drum resonates like a hollow womb.

In the field the drum is bleeding as the goat is killed and its skin stretched ever tighter, tenser, sealing the wooden womb for battle. As we prepare ourselves, we feel the pain.

The skin is stretched tighter still. We paint our faces, put on masks. We're in the jungle, here where we truly belong, Paradise Lost became a capitalist concrete jungle.

But what the fuck, we have plenty to rap about.

Too sweet? It's our musical colours. That is what moves their feet. So let's not confuse sweet for soul, boys. In this city - our city - the players gamble for the sweetest cards. Rhythms are worn behind disguises, the sweat of others is sampled knowingly. All those soul rebels must be turning in their graves.

But now it is back to the wood.

The drum of the hollow womb, its voice calling from over the tree tops. In death it gained a voice. My rhythm is my command. Together we move through this, like adventurers, rebels let loose in a land of dense woods and dense Words. My only greed is for music and Words - and this is no crime. It is present in the womb of every tree silently standing before you.

And silence is music too.
So we all grow and wait to evolve.
Now I feel it within me.
Breathe deeply.

The seer's breath was silvery-grey and it chased through the treetop foliage. His rhythms beat across the jungle. Hung over the rivers. His Words are singular gods.

The leaves trembled with a noise like maracas, guiros, timbales, bead shakers. Reaching a crescendo, piercing the silence like a hard-edged tambourine.

Crash.

A very fast flash of silver lightening sliced through the heavy, eerie atmosphere.

Then he plummeted into the satchel of darkness.

I listened, I listened on the watch for the sentence, for the word, that would give me the clue to the faint uneasiness inspired by this narrative that seemed to shape itself without human lips in the heavy night-air of the river. *17

El Gran Barco de la Corona - the grand ship of the crown was rocking, creaking against the silent night. Three main masts, each flying a flag, all held taut by ropes that carved up the seamless starry backdrop. The boy felt a nip in the wind and went to do up his waistcoat. He realised that during the day, scaling between deck and crow's nest, he had lost his top button. His trousers were beginning to wear thin round his buttocks.

Rumours chased along the ropes and the Captain's heels could be heard scuffing the bridge timbers as he paced backwards and forwards. Great tension settled with the Sea brume. A couple of crewmembers had pleaded that this insanity be stopped and that they go about and set the course for home. A select few, the boy included, knew that it was already too late to set that course - supplies were insufficient.

Earlier that day the Captain had announced that he was now finding patterns in 'los vientos alisios' - the trade winds, as well as in the differences between magnetic north and geographical north - 'la declinación magnética occidental'. The crew hushed. *18

'There is a magnetic deviation. As you are all aware we are guided by the North Star. It has come to my attention that the ship's magnetic compass deviates from the directions given by the North Star. These are only small deviations. Nonetheless, careful readings are required if we are to encounter the land that I speak of. I have set a course that will lead us to new lands and great discoveries. I know that this course will lead us there.'

'Remember the rewards if we find this route to the East. We are the initiators of Open-Sea navigation - the first to have spent so many days without a sighting of land. This has never before been achieved. We shall all go on to great things. As men of the Sea we must let our hearts be ruled by willpower and faith, not let mere superstition sway us in this belief. Let Providence be our saviour.'

The upper and lower decks echoed with the cheers as the crew shouted, 'Let Providence be our saviour!'

That was Saturday the twenty-second of September, at sunset. The Captain made the following entry in his diary:

We navigated thirty leagues with winds coming from the West and North-West. We hardly saw any seaweed but we did see petrels. The Westerly wind was much needed because my crew had become greatly agitated. They feared that Winds of a westerly direction were no more this far out to Sea and that they wouldn't be able, ever, to return home. For most of this day they didn't spot any seaweed. We were all very anxious, then suddenly we found some great thick clumps. *19

The boy knew well in advance that they were fast approaching land. He was the first to spot it and excitedly shouted out,
    'iTierra, Tierra!'

    Gracias Dios por los vientos alisios. *20

Heavy boots sunk into new sands.
    The crew strung together landings with enthusiasm; every disembarkation meant a great flurry of the native tribesmen and women, and much bartering - el trueque. The boy acquired a colourful hand-woven belt. Many of the crew asked after Gold, pointing at the inhabitants' jewellery and objects. 'Nucay,' was always the answer supported by a fluster of hands, back inland where the dark-green canopy loomed.
    The jungle, in spite of its looming proximity, didn't open itself out to them. From offshore the crew would stand and marvel at the greenness and thickness. As the Captain said,
    'Why would anyone wish to leave such a place?'
    Despite their greed, they feared this reference to inland.
    It was Tierra Desconocida. And perilous.

The jungle was surely a secret canopy hiding savage men of unknown numbers, both poisonous and murderous. Then there was the suffocating magnitude of the dense growth; once you were in, there might never be a way out. You were surrounded, on guard without knowing whether an enemy existed; the jungle plays terrible tricks on panicked minds, just as shadows trick the minds of the devious.

For now, they simply observed, but rot was setting in.

The wind roared through the foliage like a beast. Then hung before them, invisible yet audible, like a quivering note in some strange key.

Staring into the face of such an unknown, fingers quivered on triggers.

The Captain's diary for Sunday 21st October reads:

The biggest Island was called 'Colba' where there were many grand Sea boats and many fishermen. This was *the most beautiful Island that eyes have ever seen'*. *21. The Great Seas are very rich and rewarding for these fishermen. We weighed anchor again and the wind filled our hungry sails.

And for Monday 22nd - Sunday 28th October it reads:

After a week we arrived at a very beautiful river in Cuba with much beautiful vegetation, many birds and flowers. I went ashore towards two houses that I supposed belonged to fishermen. Everyone had fled. Inside the house I found one of those dogs that never bark. There were nets made from palms, ropes and fishhooks made of horn and harpoons of bone. Upstream, the landscape is most beautiful, with mountains like in Sicilia. The Indians speak of gold-mines in those mountains and shells in their waters: this is a good indication that there are pearls.

By night they anchored thinking of those high mountains. The peaks inspired Nucay. That Word, though they glinted with silver below the stars.

The crickets sung like a band of a million guiro players, enchanting everyone. Many took this as a sign that Providence was close at hand; Civilisation and Religion would advance - surely sufficient reason to make them rich.

They waited for morning.

I spy with my little eye - Nucay.

The day dawned with many colours. The enchantment of the crickets faded and a morning chill rustled the leaves of the *Palmas Reales*. This was the New World but seen through the eyes of the Old. And through the eyes of the Old, every flicker was a sign of something dreadful - an image of hell where, deeper into the thickness, sacrifices, painted faces, brilliant white wide teeth exposed blood-red throats eager to please terrifying gods. There was rope, torture, drums beaten with human bones, a wild savagery and demon-possession. Screams were heard above the incessant beat of many drums. Shrill and chilling; must be blocked out with hands covering ears.

Nucay, Nucay whispered the wind.

They were on the move, strung out in an orderly line following the embankment of a fast-flowing clean and deep river: forever onwards, upstream, uphill towards riches.

There was an abundance of rich vegetation: cotton, aloe,

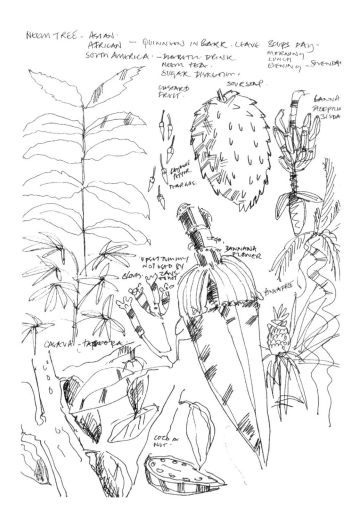

NEEM TREE - ASIAN.
ASIAN — QUININ IN BARK. LEAVE SOUPS DAY.
SOUTH AMERICA. —DIABETIC DRINK   MORNING
NEEM TEA.   LUNCH
SUGAR DISRUPTION.   EVENING —SEVENDAY

CUSTARD   SOURSOP.
FRUIT.

CAYENNE   BANANA
PEPPER.   PASOPILLA
TEAR GAS.   31 SIDA

                    BANANANA
                    FLOWER

'UPSET TUMMY
NOT USED BY
CLOVES. TANS.   PINEAPPLE
        POT NOT.

CASAVA - TAPIOCA.

COCO A
NUT.

red peppers... But still the mountain wind whispered the Word Nucay. Nothing could clear their minds of this. The Word drew them upward and deeper into unknown territory, further from the Sea that licked the shores. They were poisoned in paradise. The 'men from the sky' had brought their politics: the great lie of exploitation in the guise of philanthropy.

One step more, one fear overcome, one more thing to see, one more trick upon the imagination: a tree trunk oozing with red resin - was it a body strung upside down? A Parrot twitching on a branch - was it a face painted for war?

Or for a sacrificial ceremony?

No one spoke, but neither was there a moment's silence.

Pulses rang loud in ears: drums, drums, mystery drums.

'What do they want?' shouted one of the crew, spinning in all directions on his tired feet. In a moment of total confusion a shot ripped through the foliage - without leaving a trace. Calm was quickly restored. A rip, a rag and a panic - the guns rapidly reloaded.

They gathered upon a huge rock. The sun beat down. They turned looking around them, struck by their utter smallness and vulnerability. The rock lay sleeping like the still countenance of an Indian - could they presume him a peaceful one? The water thundered past them showering sweet spray. The fragrance was mossy, yet fresh with oily leaves and petals, cleaning the bitter smoke of gunpowder.

The boy was no longer enjoying this. Gone was the Man's World of ship and crow's nest retreat. He noticed the loss of command, he slipped like the rest through the undone net of authority. He should have remained on board or at least confined his exploration to a Boy's World on the shoreline.

Then there really were drums beating on the Wind. Everyone heard them, from the direction of the mountaintops, descending with the violence of the rapids. They cowered as if the eagle's talons were closing in on them; they heard the eagle's hunger howling in the resistance of the air under his wings, his war cry shrill, piercing the membrane between alive and dead as if you would still hear him whilst being eaten.

Uncertain of what exactly had them in its sights they panicked again and fled from their exposed position on the open rock into the cover of the jungle canopy.

The tropical storm ambushed them - just like that. The men, being superstitious, decided to heed this warning. They talked uneasily amongst themselves, their conversations trying to ride above the pounding of heavy raindrops. They gathered together under dense vegetation - this was where the jungle wished them to be.

As quickly as the storm arrived, it departed and the sun followed immediately thereafter. Steam rose from the foliage like a richly scented Turkish bath. Dancing girls swirled in between channels of bluish light, thighs green with youth. The leaves expanded and twisted in the steamy vapours, flickers of sunlight and breaths of air: the jungle was breathing. The peaks cleared and sparkled. Paradise Lost once again glinted with the promise of riches...

The warning was quickly forgotten. It was up and no hesitations this time.

No sooner had they set off than the trickery recommenced. Silvery steam enveloped the trees. The jungle was an inhospitable environment and now it was smoking - just like the inhabitants of this strange World! They were in there, too many of them! They all sat there dumbly smoking that herb they called 'Cohiba', just watching and waiting for its effects to take shape.

'Look, over there,' shouted one of the crew.

'There was smoke. I saw it too,' exclaimed another.

'And look in there.'

'Another spiral over there.'

'God have mercy on our souls!'

'Mercy on our souls,' - a response as if in prayer.

The Captain was the first to arrive at a mighty confluence in the river. The thickness of the jungle canopy dropped right down to the riverbank and leaned weightily over into the river. From now on they would be forced to penetrate the foliage further and this inspired greater fears. The Captain felt a deep anxiety for their safety, now harbouring the suspicion that they were reaching a point of no return.

With one hand on his hip, the other twisting his hair, he stood in contemplation as the others came alongside him. All eyes were wide open; they were alert and pensive. The scenery was indeed "the most beautiful that eyes had ever seen".

In that moment of breathtaking beauty, as anxiety turned to electricity, as they stood speechless and awe-struck, a rumble of thunder echoed along the valley. A shadow raced over the tops of the trees and then the call was made.

The men from the sky must return there.
And soon.
These gods that had outstayed their welcome.

The Captain heard a whining in the air increasing in pitch and intensity as it drew closer. A thud in his chest forced him several steps backward. An arrow had slipped between two of his ribs. No point to wrench it out, moving through his system was a poison. Moments later he was gripped by cramps and dark brown blood leaked from the corners of his mouth. He fell with his hand gripping the arrow as if he was clinging to the mast of his ship.

They all fell. The boy turned on the spot trying to focus on the bifurcation of the river and the peaks beyond. The sweeping blue sky swooped down on him as if to pick him up. But no, he felt weak and dizzy and was forced on to his knees. He slid over the moist rocks, down, and was taken out to Sea by a raging river; his eyes still wide with the discovery of the 'New World' but full of Old World commentaries.

Miraculously, he never swelled nor sank to the bottom of the Sea. He floated in the very bosom of the Sea always facing upwards at the sky, as a witness. There he floated and from there he observed the repeated historic process of emergence and recession - accompanied by the rhythm of the Sea.

Many years later, they found a study of the boy in the ship's logs and diaries. A woodworker found inspiration for a carving. It was donated to the future governor of the Island. It bore an uncanny resemblance.

'Tierra, Tierra'.

The Words echoed in the blackness of the Fisherman's dream. Then he thought of the satchel. He imagined it trembling from inside, restless, holding living organs and the spirit of the seer. He was not gone just yet. Once again he was emerging from the gull's shadow, from under the gull's taut wingspan. He rose away from the rotting hulls and scuttling degenerates.

His eyes suddenly opened. Wide.

It was late afternoon, but the moon was already up in position and immense. The clouds to the North hung dirty and ominous. Everything was as it had been the first morning.

Although not quite the same.

He had scored a poem into the sand and later he had realised that he was not alone, that many other people had passed through this place - it was crowded, brimming with echoes and revelations.

He looked his poem over and said,

'I never wrote that. It can't have been me.'

He turned on the spot. Just a single turn but it brought on a heavy dizziness, as when a boy stepping down from the horse carousel at the village fair. He drew a deep breath trying to control things. Then he exhaled. Then another long and steady breath in. Then out.

The motion of the waves matched his breathing pattern. He couldn't break the pattern from his mind. He looked away towards the horizon. Then he focused on the white foamy lips of the waves: Up - Inhale. Retreat - Exhale. Fortuna – Eleanora.

Nothing had changed. He had barely moved more than five metres from the shoreline during all his time here. He went over to his beloved skiff. Tears welled in his eyes; moist Mother of Pearls. He ran his dry cracked hands over the dry cracked planking and wept. The tears fell onto the decking with a soft melody like a thumb piano. He could not believe that his life at Sea and as a Fisherman was over. He slammed his fist down on the edge plank and said,

'Never again will we go out. All those times saying that this was to be 'the last fish'. But we never could escape the Majesdad del Azul Salvaje. Her beauty pulled us in, her nets of fine silver thread. And now that moment has crept up. It has come to this - wreckage and a beat old man.'

The simplicity of the skiff's construction struck him. How could he have landed all those big catches in such a boat? Now the handle and the rudder were missing, snapped at the vertical joint, stressed timbers protruded like a jagged grin.

'Men like me are born free. I have cast many nets and pulled them in - all of them but the last one. Each casting has been a new experience and every line sunk deep into the Sea's heart has captured my imagination. I have learnt so much from this great openness. Where can I possibly go from here?'

He looked into the glowing ochre sky for a moment. There was a feeling of utter exhaustion, of relief in the air as when a truce has been achieved after a long struggle.

The sun was falling, falling, steadily fall

ing.

Then he Knew what he had to do; return to History Rock, and with the last of his failing strength, to chisel out a figure in the rock column. He had an overwhelming desire - like an instruction - to leave something of permanence behind.

He no longer had the strength to swim, so he turned onto his back and floated towards the rock with small movements of his hands, like a polyp, with a simple grace. And his imagination continued unhindered. Total blueness. Time was no longer just a series of events.

A music flowed over and around him, intricately beautiful, complex beyond his understanding. It was ethereal, the rhythm hypnotic. In between the beat of two waves was a pure moment's stillness - a finely trained soft voice held a high note. It seemed to guide him beyond all the frontiers of life that he had so far experienced. The only indication of life was the pulsation of his hands as they opened and closed.

He had now pierced the hazy blue atmosphere and was travelling on a shimmering silver sword through a sharp blackness. Explosions of music were carried to him from far away, so grand and wide reaching that you could locate no source. He was travelling at a tremendous speed but there was no resistance. The notion of his movement was found in a trail that dispersed in silvery threads. No horizon, no landmarks, no shoreline. No measurements. He was everywhere. There was no destination. He was truly unshackled now, freed in a dimension of pure music of which his ignorance was total. He had nothing to fear, not a single Word to place on an emotion.

Suddenly the pulsing pattern was disturbed. The Sea swelled unpredictably round the rock that ruptured the uniformity. A wave swept over his face, and up his nose; he turned in the water and pulled himself out of the Sea coughing. The pressure dropped on him. He was all aches and pains: real and brutal and poetic again.

He sat on the rock's edge, breathing with the Sea again...

Steady, In – Out,

In, Out,

...rolled the wash and retreat of the waves. The Fisherman wished to be with them, to roll away to wherever they originated and returned to. They broke on the rock and showered him in spume.

He thought he heard voices,

'Breathe deeper, man of the Sea.'

'Breathe deeper.'

'Concentrate your strength.'

There was a brief moment of stillness and then came more waves crashing into the rock and showering him in language,

'There is work to be done.'

'Look to the sun.'

'Much work still to be done.'

The Fisherman's mouth began to move up and down in an uncontrollable manner, his lips juddering in an outpouring of psychic babble,

'I see you boy, that eye, imperishable bliss, silver sword, fish, palm of my hand, Cocuyos weave lights, purple back, I cannot reply, so alienated, never a plenitude, never a line, listen old man, let me tell you, there was never such a time....'

The babble trailed away and the Sea's silence cut through to him again. In a calm manner he concluded,

'Never a time that I stopped loving you.'

In - steady.
Out - steady.

His breathing was more controlled, deeper, steadier and in time with the guiding rhythm of his life - the motion of the Sea.

He ran his fingers roughly through his hair pulling on the roots so that his head tingled with sharp warmth. The red rays of evening shimmered across the silver-blue ocean. The old man extended his palms moving them gradually upwards until he cradled the sun. There, in his palms he held it.

This was one of the moments he treasured.

'Man cannot touch you, and I am happy to know that. Read my palms and you will see that I too am made of inexhaustible poetry. I have known what it is to hunt, the cunning and the suffering involved. In my quest I became the hunted, every turn I made towards survival took me closer to surrender. No longer do I seek. Before you, I lay down my tradition, I rest my hands, raw from a lifetime's labour.'

The Fisherman continued to hold out his palms and stare into the diminishing sun. For a moment he saw his ancestors working and living in peace: their children running free. His father was standing and reading to an attentive crowd, his mother sat straddled over a rounded ridge separating two mountain valleys. His fellow fishermen were chatting as they tended to their nets. Nobody was speechless. Everyone belonged in a making of song, earth and labour.

In the red was a Hope, one that he had been invited to

share. He was being drawn down with the sinking sun. His hands now felt heavy. He brought them down slowly to his sides, never taking his eyes off the sun as it inched downwards. His mother was still there saddling the mountains; she looked at her son, telling him not to worry anymore. There was a brief warm gust of mountain air across the Sea as she blew him a kiss, and she was gone.

The entire horizon blushed.

He felt wretched and weak and a longing to depart.

But the Love and the Hope are all in the waiting.

He turned and scrambled to the top of the rock. He looked around him again. He was struck by the beauty and grandeur. The Sea rolled out in a black and blue carpet before him, the sky seemed to join the Sea at its furthest point and then return as a thin sheet to cover him. The small bay hung in the background like a painting in a gallery, closed for the day and with the lights out.

His attention was seized by some movement across the sand. He made himself blink and stared harder. He was right. There was movement. A liquid was flowing in the score lines of his Words like lava along a river-bed.

'Upon this broken ground' ... He blinked again. The beach was still. His poem glowed silver. It was like viewing a reflection in a mirror whose back had been badly scratched. For a moment it seemed the Words had a life of their own, a separate value, fed by arteries from a living and vital source. Exactly where the poem had emerged from surprised the Fisherman, but he had since distanced himself from it. His Words sat among a whole collection of other scorings. The sandy space had opened itself out to creative forces and abuse. Many passers-by had invaded the space

but he couldn't escape feeling very alone. He was totally isolated, had heard no sight or sound of the Havana Coast Guard scouring the area.

Did a lifetime at Sea amount to something, or nothing, after all?

The Fisherman shrugged his shoulders and shivered. He crossed his arms and rubbed his sore palms over his upper arms and shoulders. He spoke very softly to himself from atop the rock,

'Still good this body of mine. It's my mind that lets me down.'

His courage was undoubtedly that of the hunter, his silhouette a landmark on the skyline. He was now the hunted. But his forefathers had shown him in the vision of the setting-sun that in time he would be welcomed, and this reunion would be based on song, earth and labour. Their colour was red - a full and rounded redness, at the place where his heart beat peacefully and tirelessly, far away from the massing shadow where even the rivers run without poetry of motion.

This is what he needed to express: character, tradition, expression, culture, tragic history. He needed to show it all.

Something had instructed that 'there was work to be done'.

He feared the hollowness - the insignificance that would echo over these waters if he failed to fix symbols of his independence, pride and tradition. Frustrated, he rubbed his knuckles up and down his forehead trying to force out an idea. He glanced back towards the shore. He saw that his skiff had turned nearly ninety degrees but was jerking still with the rhythm of the Sea. The visual pattern remained the same film loop winding by, only now the frames seemed to be passing in more rapid succession: the tempo was undoubtedly increasing.

The letters in the name Eleanora became readable in the silvery light. With the increased rocking motion they elongated. The letters merged and danced, spiralling upwards.

Now he could see Eleanora herself. She was writing. He just managed to read the Words *All I wanted was for your red shadow to mingle with mine. And never to depart....* Then her face filled the entire frame - a close-up but very, very far away.

There followed several frames of blackness.

The Words 'Fortuna' began to come to life. There was a man stood with a lit cigarette at a street corner. His one hand was sunk into his suit jacket, but the way he drew on the cigarette exposed some uneasiness. He leant against a cool stone doorway, above him a colourful ceramic plaque read 'IN HERE GOD PROTECTS THOSE IN NEED'. He fidgeted shifting his weight between one heel and the other.

The next scene showed cars and guns. There were bullets ripping into the man, splintering the ceramic and message of the plaque. A caption sprang out of the sand,

The portrait of bullet-ridden yesterday

From out of the confusion came a face. That face. It was the seer. He stopped and threw his gaze into the fisherman's. They were like film lenses panning hard, zooming in tight, forcing him back against the stone column. The Fisherman's cream coloured eyes looked through the seer's and saw a mist swirling. A Warning flashed in the sand.

The pull was terrific.

He raced through many vacuums to crash upon a black man's back. He could hear a voice, many voices,

'Punishment: 33, 34, 35!'

One voice rose above the swish and crack of leather straps, disembodied cries and heavenly voices,

'40 for you!'

The whip cracked across the Fisherman's own back. The sound shook him, and the pain. He looked around him frantically. A girl was crouching, cowering on a summit, very high. At a distance were others of her Culture. She was beautifully clothed, her weavings tight, colourful and noble like her breath. This high, the girl felt the pressure of her destiny. Pressure from voices, from Gods, from proximity to the heavy dusky sky.

She was to be a sacrifice to the powerful spirits that granted her people prosperity. She had no strength to flee. Where could she go? The World was much bigger then, full of great unknowns. The soil slowly filled her lungs and tomb with the promise of reward in the after-life, as the drunken singing crowd danced on. And on.

And on.

On...

Click.

The frame froze on her lowered head.

The seer flashed into the picture for a split second. Words sparkled upon her beautiful thick black hair:

We wrote no language then,
Never dig me up, or loot me, or put me on display,
I gave my life for my people,
In peace I wish to stay.

Her head began to move; as she looked upwards the Fisherman saw her decomposing skull. In her eye-sockets were two silver glints.

The frame switched to North America.

Sunlight bounced off metal tools. The men were way up, levelling, tapping, welding, walking along metal beams. They were indeed building a city in the place reserved for dreams. The World below busied by in miniature scale, the speed seemed comical. At this distance the Walking Men of Metal Beams glided serenely along the dividing lines of sanity and madness.

In the middle of one such beam, very high up, a man stood, his arms outstretched - further, outwards and upwards, until he was balancing on the tips of his toes. He held the pose with confidence; everyone around him froze.

He plunged and fell. Three metres from the ocean's surface the warm air gushed past him. The blue was so blue that he flew effortlessly, no feeling for the speed or distance. The earth's darkness would never come and sweep across such cool blue.

But it did.

The bird tired at sunset and by chance spotted a skiff belonging to a Fisherman. It landed close to the mast then jumped along to the stern in order to rest at the furthest extremity of the petit skiff, to guard as safe a distance as possible from man's reach. The Fisherman realised that he was watching himself in this film. He had spoken with the bird. This he remembered and he began to recall his Words aloud,

'So you tire, *Pájaro del Mar*, and have been forced to land on my skiff against your better judgement. You must know that I am a hunter: our relationship could go one way, or the other. But I also need a break from the solitude, the emptiness cast upon us by this night. Come, have some Peces Golondrinos from my nets and enjoy. Take your time *Pájaro del Mar,* pick away and build up your strength. I chew and chew, and like you I must look to the Sea in need of good nourishment. Why should we be at odds when we are forever at the mercy of greater things?'

He had been worn out himself. He had curled up on the deck, pushing his bare back against the planking for warmth, well below the night wind's passage. When he awoke at daybreak, the *Pájaro del Mar* was gone, as were the fish scraps, but thoughts of freedom and movement occupied his thoughts all that day.

'Yes, if my fate is to be shared with my father's, perhaps I too will take to the sky, seek out horizons, travel, rest and receive nourishment.'

Now the Fisherman closed his straining eyes wishing to end the projections but the reflections were equally as strong, only now the frames were passing quicker, chopped in one after the other, superimposed, irregularly shot, edited so quickly, confusingly and randomly. There were streets of Havana, streets of New York, bars, crystals, ladies, gentlemen, jazz cellars, paintings on walls, little black angels, masters of ceremony, domino players under trees during lazy afternoons. Also cars, flags, monuments, swirling treetops, green, green hills, beaches and children, a floating blue bottle containing unknown scented air and a white piece of paper. Palmas Reales quivering majestically, kids playing baseball on a vacant lot, lovers seated on the Sea wall, bicycles, beers, European architecture, beach combing, war boats, aeroplanes. And so many faces, bodies, statues, heroes, stained glass, graffiti on walls, castles, bridges, revolutions, boats, nets, museums, paths, jungles, loudspeakers, trains and train stations, universities, plazas, fields, sunsets, sugarcane plantations, coffee beans, crowds, leaders, microphones, musical instruments, cables in the sky, hospitals, trains, pages from books fluttering on the wind, workers in fields, fiestas, crop gatherings, cigars, mountaintops, valley walls, mumbling rivers, water catchments, swirling eddies...

The frame suddenly jammed on some numbers from a lottery board:

4474
4743
11078
11911
36716
38368

He tried to clear his mind of its rubbish collection. He failed. His mother moved in front of the numbers, laughing and sporting rolled cardboard tubes for curlers in her hair. The Fisherman heard her saying from somewhere,

'It's my little permitted weakness son - I like a gamble.'

She drew on her cigarette and exhaled slowly, facing him. Her white teeth brightened her smile. The smoke brought water to his eyes. The images quickly blurred and faded into a length of black run-off film that seemed to pop with fragments of leftover silver dust. The Fisherman coughed. Viscous bile rose in his throat and clung to the back.

He turned and went over to the stone column. He knelt before the tools and ran his fingers over the scribes, chisels and hammer. He felt a tingling sensation in his finger-tips that was instructing him to pick up the hammer and chisel and simply begin.

The hammerhead was heavy; a balanced swing required concentration. His first swing was sloppy - his left hand holding the chisel wobbled, the hammer came down off-centre. It failed to mark the surface with any real authority. He couldn't believe the poor result. He glanced up at the sky, breathing hard, muttering. This was going to be far tougher than he had ever thought. Against pain and weakness, he gritted his teeth and began to hammer away.

This initial anger showed results: stone chippings flew into the air at the bite of the chisel tip; it ripped through the stone deeply and easily. With each stroke the hammer seemed lighter, the swing more controlled and easier to judge. Beneath the outer rock layer was a cleaner and brighter surface, silvery-grey in the light of moon and stars. He remembered the voices hurtling back at him from across the Sea, slapping him in the face:

An Angel chiselled out of a block of salt...

'No, n-o, this can-not be. Please. I, I...'

He took more swings at the stone until he had taken back a considerable strip. He stopped, put the tools down and ran his finger tips over the freshly opened layers.

'I will never do this,' he thought. 'Too much has been asked of me. But I do not need to attain perfection. A simple image cut roughly will do. The Sea, the sky and their allies will fine tune the rest - polish it up for me. Why always seek perfection? Just this once, be content old man!'

He swung heavily, stripped back more surface rock. The chippings chinked on History Rock; he was aware of subtle melodies generated by these very physical rhythms. His

breathing took an off-beat from the motion of the waves,
like a staccato wind instrument: this helped him gather
momentum:
  The swing.
  The connection.
  The chink.
  The dig.
  The twist.
  The wrist.
  The loosening.
  The fall.

He had found the rhythm and sunk into it. But he was very,
very weak. The pain gnawed away at his insides. He was
roaming in the midday desert, stung awake by the sharp
cold prick of the ice flower's deadliest thorn. It had found
him, injected him with a slow poison that moved ever so
discreetly, gaining ground within him.

First Purple and Pink spots, then blackness, then a brilliance so blinding that it triggered a headache. Every tap of
the hammer was a fragment of irrecoverable life. He
realised that he was expending himself in what seemed like
a terrible punishment - as if he was being forced to carve
his own tombstone.

Once as he swung the hammer he saw a lingering flash
of the mountain girl being sacrificed on the cold summit.
His chisel dug in to the stone, his wrist loosened it and
chippings jumped out. Then her head was in front of him
with a deep and messy wound. It felt as cold as old stone.
He brushed the fine chippings away with his fingertips and
her image popped, leaving a cloud of bone dust.

He felt numbed by it all. Each loosened chunk of stone

was something lost from himself; a loss of body, of muscle and of mind. What replaced it was nothingness, blankness where there was nothing left to say. Sometimes this nothingness would have the Fisherman stop, get up and wander dazed about the rock. But every time he was drawn back to his tools and his labour, to his thoughts. And now his determination was becoming hewn in solid rock. He set to again, scoring out a design whilst the anchoring line towards destiny tugged, tightened and pulled at the threshold of his pain.

The scoring instrument was much thinner and needed to be gripped very differently than the chisel. He found this hard, his muscles too tense, and this upset him. These fingers that had threaded so many hooks and baits, repaired so many torn nets, were like claw hammers. Like the pincers of an old crab locked onto a stick.

The fisherman paused for breath to catch again the pattern in his breathing. He tried to clear his throat and said,

'I just want my fingers to be nimble and strong as before. That's not too much to ask, is it?'

The Fisherman drew in a deep breath and whispered softly on his exhaled air,

'Well, is it?'

He blanked out.

The scoring instrument fell to the ground.

His father flickered in silver threads in the darkness. Again he was reading,

The memory throws up high and dry
A crowd of twisted things;
A twisted branch upon the beach
Eaten smooth, and polished

As if the World gave up
The secret of its skeleton,
Stiff and white. *22

The World gave up. As if the World gave up. The Fisherman
could hear these Words spinning somewhere in the darkness. From out of nowhere they were hurtling towards him.

He saw a beached whale skeleton rattling in the wind;
ringing with the impact of airborne grains of sand.

'Find a voice, find a voice,' he cried.

An old crab waved a fattened stiff claw at him, trying to
lock onto one of his fingers. Its black-ball eyes bounced
like oily suspension springs. This startled him back to con-
sciousness. He found himself pressed against the stone.

He scrambled awkwardly down the side of the rock to
where it met the Sea. He found a ledge slightly under the
surface and sat down with his bottom and legs submerged.

He was suffering tremendously. He put his hands and
arms into the Sea to wash off the small fragments of stone.
The saltwater stung his palms. The wounds from the deep
cast lines had been reopened by the stone carving.

The Sea was still. So still.

'What was that?'
'What did you say?'

Not a sound.

'So, why have you nothing to say?'

'There is music in silence too,' remembered the
Fisherman. 'Silence is a precious sound, semi-precious,
perhaps like mother of pearl.'

He paused and sighed.

It started with a flicker, a flash from the deep that triggered a fine-traced series of notes. Thousands and thousands of voices swam from the deep singing in harmonies that varied so little in pitch that they could be an incantation. Voices and lights increased in volume. From a single sparkle of silver there were suddenly thousands of individual phosphorescent plankton moving steadily upward towards where the Fisherman had plunged his tired muscles, his sore and bleeding palms.

They came directly to his hands, a shower of tiny anaesthetic pinpricks. The Fisherman was amazed. Never had he dreamt of such magic; so simple, so silver and sweet. The phosphorescent bodies had always come to him by night.

The Fisherman felt humbled by this extraordinary gift of the Sea. He slowly opened and closed his fingers with a new vigour, swishing his hands amid the phosphorescent trails.

The Sea felt warm and full, still and musical - as a tingling celebration of life:

All life began in the Sea.

Among the tiny silver splinters of life, a long slender underwater shadow passed in front of the rock. By the moonlight he could just distinguish a purplish streak and a beautiful strong back. There was a sound like a cello string bowed. It hovered back and forth over the one note, a quivering vibrato. It wasn't menacing, more moody. The tempo was slow and purposeful, waiting for some grand finale.

The waves broke without further clues. They had simply demystified themselves and become waves - relentless and seemingly pointless comparisons to this evocative nightfall.

The Fisherman thanked the phosphorescent plankton and sat further up on the ledge, looking now at the sky. The dark cloud from the North was spreading and also losing height - but it still appeared a long way off.

The Fisherman turned his attention to the moon.

'You seem much closer this night, full of charm and secrets,' he said.

A thin cloud whispered around her. The Fisherman coughed. A terrible internal pain punched the inside of his swollen stomach.

'Neither of us is too good. And we are both old now,' he muttered.

But the moon didn't respond - she'd seen it all before. She was bored and preferred to smooth the face of the Sea. This was more interesting, more narcissistic, on the Sea she saw her reflection as forever changing variations on a theme: always with an air of magic, always a witness to what the sun and the tired eyes of this World never see.

The Fisherman looked hard at her reflection on the Sea and saw her rippling towards him, then he blinked and she was crouching on the back of a wave like a silver coin in a black man's hand. She could be flipped over by those big hands. Their half-moon nails were her only surprises. She smiled flirtatiously at earth's aged corners.

'Yes, she's a trickster – a rough Señora who thinks she's an angel, then a goddess in the same instant. She's nothing but a frail old lady whose powdered face is so heavily made-up that she chokes on her puff powder until it tumbles down the craters and shows her for what she is - an old hag,' chattered the Fisherman.

Once spluttered out, these ill words surprised him. He coughed heavily. Thick blood surfaced on his lips and crept down the lines that the sun had worked on him over many long years. The blood had the effect of soothing his temperament. It changed his mood. He saw that getting worked up now was not going to bring any peace of mind. And that was precisely what he had come to desire from the whole irreversible experience.

He dropped his voice to a softer level,

'You're kinder to me in this hour than I could imagine, and for that I thank you, for you have seen much suffering and mine cannot amount to much. You carry many of our burdens, counter our negative energies and tuck them safely away. Maybe you were wild, alive and beautiful once, but this work bled you until you were a dead dusty ball.'

He stared into the Sea.

One wave, or a countless number?

Who knows?

A bottle chinked against the rock, a hard repetitive single note varying only in rhythm and volume. It was blue, a wine bottle, half-corked. Perhaps there was a drinkable liquid inside? The Fisherman held it up to the moon but it was empty - except for a crumbly, cream-coloured paper.

'You. It is you that has done this to me,' said the Fisherman shaking the bottle angrily at the moon.

But the bottle had the air of a treasure chest, something that had escaped from the bottom of the Sea, from the bed of history's rotting hulls, broken tongues and scavengers. Even if it had never been as far down as those dreadful places, it had spent a lifetime bobbing between two Worlds, forever en-route.

He tucked it into his trouser waist and scaled the side of the rock to where his final task was scattered before him.

The Cocuyos still cast their little lights.

He   placed the bottle to one side of the column.

Pain. It was pure pain. He tensed all his muscles as a cramp crazed his stomach and held on to him. It wouldn't let go. He was digesting acid; the walls were dissolving and the openness was coming in. Grey first. Then black. He passed out. But this time the blackness was fractured by a powerful and brilliant light.
And a voice followed,

And the voice which I heard from heaven spake unto me again, and said, Go and take the little book which is open in the hand of the angel which standeth upon the sea and upon the earth.
And I went unto the angel, and said unto him, Give me the little book. And he said unto me, Take it and eat it up; and it shall make thy belly bitter, but it shall be in thy mouth sweet as honey.
And I took the little book out of the angel's hand, and ate it up; and it was in my mouth sweet as honey: and as soon as I had eaten it, my belly was bitter. *23

When the Fisherman came round he found his head propped up against the stone column. He could feel a steady pain stabbing above his left eye and the heat of abrasion across his cheek. But pain was now too distant to be of any immediate consequence. He gripped the stone with his working palms and righted himself.
'I've had a terrible dream,' the Fisherman suddenly figured. 'An angel standing upon the Sea with a little book, and me, with my belly bitter and my mouth sweet. Only books and Words to eat.'
Fragments of his scored beach poetry flashed at him like a light bulb being turned on and off repeatedly in a darkened room. His eyes blurred with the afterglow.

Words emerged:

So beautifully bone white - like --
An Angel chiselled out of a block of salt.

He blinked. Yes, there were many Angels flashing out at Sea tonight. In the blink of an eye, one appeared right in front of him. He made out the profile of a man discussing something with the Angel, although he couldn't be too sure, it might have been a woman rolling in a weighty wave. It, he, she, all was fantastic, and the Fisherman knew that his mind was playing tricks. The Angel dropped behind into the shadow of another powerful wave and he felt naked and denied.

If only there was someone with whom to share his emotions, to break this deafening solitude where crowds, apparitions and voices were choirs whose voices hung in the church air long after they had vacated the pews.

But of course someone might really be coming. Fellow fishermen would find him, or a Coastguard would spot his skiff from the air. This is why he hadn't moved. And of course he believed himself special, a protégé of the *Majesdad del Azul Salvaje* herself.

Right now, in this battered and bruised state, it was the solitude that was beginning to hurt much more than the thirst, the hunger, the cuts and multiple bruises. Perhaps the working of this stone was a futile task.

'I am just doing this to kill time, take my mind away from all the suffering and many voices of the Sea,' he thought on many occasions.

Yet how could he explain the visions? How could he explain the boy appearing, the poems, his poem, the crowds, the voices, the satchel and the implements that his father had described to him? Why was he tied to this place if he was so free? Why had no Coastguard spotted him? Why hadn't a single person come down to this beach?

The voices had first called him back into existence. He hadn't felt completely alone. He sheltered some hope: there was the Sea opening out before him and she would bring help and assistance - fellow fishermen, a passing vessel, a Coastguard. But could any of them really have saved him? He had suffered a terrific test of endurance at Sea and it had sapped nearly all his fighting spirit.

The Sea had lent him time to find himself further, to consider history, to reflect on his life and achievements. During these two drawn out days, he saw that he had travelled far. His outbursts of aggression and disillusionment of self and spirit could be forgiven. With his soul roots, he had developed a belief in his life, his tradition, his freedom, his character in the openness.

He wasn't ever alone after all. He had seen his people in the reddened disk of the setting sun. His father had read to him again. They had consoled him and put away his fear of being just another tormented voice blowing over a level expanse without any destination. The sun had dropped below the horizon, blood red as his heart beat grew slower and heavier. It resounded in his ears - deep like marching boots over oak flooring.

'Colours. All these wonderful colours,' the Fisherman had once said to his son. 'Eyes are so precious, like mother of pearl, you turn one in your hand and in every different angle you find a new colour. Did I tell you that I have looked in to the eye of the Sea? I peered down deep - deeper than any old eye can see. I prised open the shell and found her looking at me. Eyes are telling of so much. Often before a Word is spoken, all is told just in the eyes. When they are alive with the greatness of life, they have a silvery coating of moisture over them - just like the Sea, just like the stars, just like the moon and this rich vegetation after rain. For this reason son, silver is my favourite colour - a true friend, even by night, a friend for life.'

The Fisherman was enveloped in silver - it bounced along the Sea towards him, was worn by the moon and was elegantly strung like a necklace in the stars of the sky. His poem on the beach glinted in silver threads and the silver phosphorescent bodies were faithful to his every touch. The Fisherman's energy was silver, as was the eye of the Sea. Silver had become his colour of faith, trust and meaning. It was his heart of silver that beat life and hope in these dark hours.

He sat before the stone column. He stared into the night, into the blackness and beyond the stars until his eyes could travel no more. His vision blurred. When finally he blinked he was startled by what he saw. A silver trail joined up the stars and formed an image.

The Fisherman marvelled at it. He blinked again - hard and firm to be sure that it wasn't another mind play. He squeezed his sore palms, rubbed his forehead and felt the pain of his existence. It was still there - strong and definitive amongst a wash of silver fragments. What he saw was a muscular forearm, obviously tensed as the fingers were tightly turned in and tendons and veins protruded sharply from out of the muscle. The hand was curled around a long slender fish that had a mark of strangeness about it, as well as beauty and confidence. Its most noticeable peculiarity was that its eye was at an odd angle on its head. The

grip looked as if it was at man's mercy and yet it was obvious that this fish was the master of the great Seas.

'The boy,' recalled the Fisherman, 'he's alive. I know he
is. It was he who told me again that all life comes from the
Sea. He asked me to bring him here so that he could tell
me his story and to show me all these things. I brought him
and lost him. He was too heavy and I too feeble - not my
fault. But now he's looking down again. He never has really left me.'

The Fisherman's intake of breath suddenly shortened and
he stopped mumbling to catch some rapid breaths. His
breathing hissed like the gush of air under the wings of a
huge bird. He controlled it until it eased ever so slightly.

He looked around him, swinging his head round as best
he could, his eyes focusing around the rock and out at Sea.
There was no boy. He looked again to the sky and saw that
the eye of the fish resembled the one that had looked up
from the deep Sea as he peered down below from his skiff.

The Fish's body arched. And where it met with the man's
fingers there was an outstretched dorsal fin, sharp and
bony. The bones passed between the man's fingers like
long rigid spears. The tips of the fins and a part of the
Fish's back were shaped into the rooftop profile of his village. The man's forearm was held vertically aloft but the
Fish was gripped at a forty-five degree angle.

The Fisherman recognised all these elements. He
exclaimed,

'My people, the Sea, the seer, the sun, the sky, the
poems, my father, the Words - they are instructing me to
carve this into the stone. The shape is right. I can do this!
I must be strong like I have always been.'

He reached for the scribe and began to score out elements of the Fish's head all the time referring to the silvery trail hanging high in the sky. The Fisherman guided the scribe to place it differently, but he felt his hand working away from his line. His fingers were disobeying him. He scratched and chipped away as instructed and the head and eye quickly took shape.

Once the head was correct the silvery trail began to disappear like an overgrown country path. There was only his memory now to refer to. Nonetheless, the image was strong and the trails had momentarily lived in his eyes. He could have reproduced it blind. He adored the approach run to his village; the beach growing by the second, his nets in, his skiff teeming with silver fish and the shadowed rooftops comforting sleepy heads, trapping dreams. It brought a smile to the Fisherman's lips. Yes, this was how he loved to look from afar at his pueblo as the warm South-westerly trade winds - los vientos alisios - pushed him steadily on towards the shore.

'I am so close to home,' thought the Fisherman. 'Now my people think of me, they wonder what became of me. And yes, you too Eleanora, listen to this pleasant warm wind as now I am replying.'

The Fisherman began to swing the hammer and drive the chisel into the stone, the loosened fragments flying off and chinking on the stone and against the bottle.

He had found a fresh hope and new energy.

The Sea responded to his vigour by throwing up waves of an increasing strength. But they weren't storm waves. He could smell the air - there was no storm brewing. It was strange that the Sea should respond so dynamically to his energy. He felt like a magnet drawing in molecular chaos.

He drove the chisel in further, the tip biting into the stone, then the twisting and the chippings falling loosely all around him. He was a worker - his hands were his faithful servants. He worked the chisel well; and with all work of this nature, progress seems slow, but the moment you relax into it and find a steady rhythm, the signs of progress are soon everywhere around you.

His thoughts carried him off but they always returned to the task in hand.

'All this life would be incomplete without any reference to it,' reckoned the Fisherman. 'I have learnt the inadequacy of Words, the roughness of mortal speech. I have experienced more here than I can and care to express. When a god passed before me, my father told me that he was the Word - but no one spoke to him and he didn't utter a single syllable. Words failed even him. God as the Word was wordless and just as helpless as I am now - A Man of the Sea without a boat is what I have become. I may as well be a fish without a Sea, or a star without energy in the sky. But none of this matters now - this monument will echo with time like the stones of the Lost City. Yes, without it I would be incomplete. Speech - l - e - s - s.'

The fisherman felt a sharp pain under his breath. All he could do was to inhale very short and rapid breaths. The hammer slipped from his hand and the Fisherman hugged the stone. But this wasn't going to help. He could feel his blood thick in his veins; his heart was clogging up with its viscosity.

He lay flat on his back and deathly still to ease the pressure. He knew that he had gone beyond his means. That same series of events flashed through his mind: endless hours at Sea, wrestling with a fish, with a line that cut deep; bent back, riddled cramps into old body, out too far, so very, very, very far, I'm afraid. Terrible thirst, terrible storm, struggled with the boom, the rudder snapped - gone, ducking to avoid a blow to head, bucket after bucket, bailing out seawater. How futile - one scoop, one dig at the might of a storm-whitened Sea, swinging boom, duck, too late and over and out.

The Fisherman's chest pain left him and he began to chuckle at the thought.

'How could a single old man bail out the ferocity of that Sea, who chose to show herself in the pride of her strength? I am old and stubborn. I told the Fish that we would both suffer the consequences. We simply fought too hard, resisted one another for too long, went too far out and the Sea punished us for our stupidity, for our old and obstinate ways. Now...'

The Fisherman stopped to catch his breath,

'...we both are dying in much the same way, and thinking of the other. What became of you my beautiful proud friend? The storm never got you just as it didn't get me. The Sea took mercy on us both. With your line loosened, you dived to freedom where more peaceful waters flow. I can see you now Fish. You can't escape me even now.'

He lifted his head up and saw the Fish's form taking shape in the stone. Its fin was sticking through the fingers of the tensed hand.

'That was your way of saying to me, if I must go, then you must come with me. You will have been hungry like me after days of wrestling the line, after pulling the weight of my skiff. But the struggle will have disorientated you, made you too weak to hunt for food and in unfamiliar waters. You will have slowed right down, stared into the dark depths of our *Majesdad del Azul Salvaje* and spent your time thinking, seeing, listening, sensing and resting. To rest - how much we both need to rest now, Fish!'

'I have known you, Fish, through my sufferings - they are now equal to yours. All is equal again, as it was before I met you. And you were right to fight and show me this. I am glad that we shall go together. I should have listened to you then. I could see you moving slowly, peaceful waters across your back - only now you are lying weak like me and starting to turn to one side, your gills moving faster and faster. Every time that you correct yourself it hurts that little bit more. Am I not right, Fish? Every time it hurts that little bit more. Now I must correct myself too. Make that last stand and show what I have learnt from you.'

The Fisherman raised himself to his elbows - ever so slowly. His heart thumped that little bit deeper and sonorous, his blood heavy. Much less was now finding its way to his brain. The drums, the rhythm, the natural swing were all fading. The end would have to be free-styled, ad-libbed - it's true that such an ending cannot be rehearsed.

It must be a melody unlike any other.

Once sat cross-legged in front of his sculpture with the hammer and chisel in his hand, the Fisherman paused and felt the tug towards a blackness, like a fish tempting the bait. He knew that there would be no more temptation, there would not be another torch emerging from the blackout to show him the exit. He caught the plunge in time and flicked his head towards the Sea - the sudden movement recharged him.

The waves were calmer now, speaking the moment. They were softly uttering the many languages of the shores that they had visited: onomatopoetic Words were hummed against the rock. The Fisherman could hear their tones. He felt drawn to their softness. He was in a half-dream state wanting to succumb to their caresses and flowing peace. But his determination kept building a wall between the Sea and himself. He had to find that strength and complete what everyone had asked of him.

The encroaching peace was pushed back with each swing of the hammer. The noise of the metal head upon the metal shaft rang out into the night; a series of lonely chimes like bells from a high Andean monastery. The scattering of the loose chippings sounded like the first layers of a road under construction that would lead believers up to its doors. This is how the Americas were built.

The Fisherman's sculpture was now showing more shape. The rooftop of the pueblo emerged, as did the fingers and the man's hand. The forearm took on human dimensions. Swing after swing,

The connection.
The chink.
The dig.
The twist.
The wrist.
The loosening.
The fall.

2 times. 7 times. 23 times. 349 times. 2305 times...

He began to sense the turn. Daybreak was coming, even if there were still many hours in between.

These revolutions are precise.

A huge fish glided ever-so-slowly by. It was circling the rock as 'the Fish' had circled the skiff. His body was a long slender dark shadow and beautiful to watch. The early hour, the darkened blue of the Sea and the smoothness of the Fish's movements gave the scene a gloomy perfection. But what really startled the Fisherman was the singular glint in its eye. He looked again, focusing harder. At that moment he saw a bolt of silver light run the length of the magnificent body. The Fish had turned towards the sky, then slowly righted itself.

'My God,' said the Fisherman aloud. 'That Fish is dying.'

He watched it loop the rock several times more.

Now he noticed that the Sea around the rock - around himself - was beginning to fill with fish. It was swelling and their mass and movements, their presence, could be felt vibrating through the rock. He tapped away some more at the stone, conscious that his heart was now groaning like a ship's hull wedged in between the tightening jaws of a ruthless ice-floe.

The Fisherman's chiselling was now more frantic and without rhythm. He would pause often and lean over to one side on his elbow so as to level his chest off a fraction. His heart thumped in his ears like orchestral Timpani - booming in the crucial places.

He breathed slowly in.

Then out.

Around him there was a gathering: Cocuyos, waves, wind, stars and rising light. The Sea was agitated. Thousands and thousands of fish were being drawn to the rock. The moon's reflection was now more fragmented than ever - the thousands of fins and tails sent out irregular currents.

These currents swept into the rock and broke into a hum

of voices chattering enthusiastically like a well attended party. He thought he could catch the odd Word in between his heavy hammer-blows. No sentences, the voices were muffled and unclear - quite unlike in his visions and dreams. The thud of his heart had overpowered all the other sounds.

'That Fish,' said the Fisherman, 'circles this rock like a timekeeper round a clock face. Only he is moving anti-clockwise. Maybe he swims with the swell. I do not know what course a fish decides on. But he is watching me close-ly from all angles. He never takes that singular eye off me. Does he hold me responsible for his suffering? Or are we to be friends?'

There was a sudden stillness.

It was tremendously tense.

The Fisherman shivered. It ran all through his body and didn't cease. He spoke with a shaky voice,

'So, Fish, soon the muscles in my arms will have been expended into stone. Then we shall see how we are to be. I know that I am not any better than you.'

The Fisherman raised his weary arm again and let the hammer drive into the chisel head. Now he was privileging the muscles and veins on his sculpture: his own were burn-ing, on the point of escaping like molten lava from a fis-sure. His back, normally straight and tight with proud strong shoulders, now arched like a rainbow and his heavy head was drooping like a young palm tree after a storm.

He saw fuzzy shades of brown around the edges of his vision. There were also spots of silver and white. Where exactly they came from, he wasn't sure. But he took his gaze up to the sky and thought he saw a satellite moving between the stars.

Nothing was sharp anymore. Even the stars seemed vague. The Fisherman tried to focus on the North Star. Instead he met with the clouds of uniformity.

'They are closer,' he figured. 'Or am I farther?'

Then his attention was caught by a splash in the Sea.

'You are so big. A real master of the ocean,' said Fisherman to Fish.

It had rolled over again onto its side and floated amongst the teeming others, yet strangely distant from the shoal, just as the old seer had been when he walked with the crowd over History Rock.

The Fisherman went to make another swing with the hammer.

Somewhere in the motion he was carried forwards and for a split second he saw a Purple-Pink bubble the size of a hot air balloon burst in his eyes. The hammer slipped from his bleeding and mushy palm, the chisel swivelled and his knuckles scraped down the sculptured stone. The chisel fell from his clutch, hit the bottle, breaking it and scattering the shouts of a million voices. The paper blew, dropped and floated on the Sea.

He fell back onto his elbows and faced his sculpture. There would be no more finishing touches. What he saw now before him was his work in solid stone.

'The Sea and wind will polish this for me,' he decided. 'What do you say, Fish?'

He turned his head and focused on the Fish's side.

The Fish was still turned, showing a long slender silver body with a streak of Purple. His tail quivered ever so slightly. He was still formidable.

'You are so noble my friend. Please do not lie like that, looking intensely at me. Right yourself and swim out. Do not wait for me. Go whilst you can. I am already gone. We will meet later. Finally, I give you my Word. You no longer have any reason to doubt me. Do not die Fish! Please, do not die in this way. Listen to me.'

The Fisherman looked away - out to Sea, but could no longer see clearly through his moist mother of pearl eyes. He breathed deeply, gathered some strength in his lungs and called, tenderly,

'Do not die Fish. Swim! Just right yourself and swim. Why won't you listen to me?'

The Fish suddenly righted itself. There was a small splash.

But it didn't move.

In an instant an incredible and penetrating silence overwhelmed the Fisherman. The Sea's agitation froze. Not a wave rose to break against the rock. Not a fish flicked a fin.

Just,

- Silence -

The sudden cessation of motion was startling. Everything respected it. Even the Sea stilled its monotonous ticking-away of Time.

This was abnormal, supernatural. The Fisherman was witnessing a miracle. He wasn't sure what to do or where to look. He turned his head in all directions and noticed the sky had changed to a lighter blue. The day was pouring in around the stars. The silver was slightly tarnished with Purple.

The Fisherman withdrew into the silence.

There he saw the boy before him, to the side of the sculpture. The boy said clearly,

'We cannot think of a time that is oceanless.'

'What does this mean?' thought the Fisherman. 'Oceanless?'

'Time the destroyer is time the preserver,' came an echo.

The Fisherman paused in thought, then gently placed his Words,

'So what am I witnessing at this moment? A time that is oceanless? This ragged rock no longer sits in the restless waters.'

'The Sea has many voices.'

'There is music in silence too.'

'Many Gods and many voices.'

'So now let us listen.'

The Fisherman closed his eyes and listened, dead still, in front of his statue.

The Fish rolled over onto its side and looked upwards from within the *Majesdad del Azul Salvaje.*

* NOTES *

1. *Palmas Reales*: Palm Trees most prominent in Cuba, as referred to by explorer-botanist Alexander Von Humboldt in his *Personal Narrative Of A Journey To The Equinoctial Regions Of The New Continent.*

2. Hemingway, Ernest, *THE OLD MAN AND THE SEA*, Arrow Books, 1993, p.80.
The author met the 'Old Man' of 'The Sea' - *Gregorio Fuentes* in person whilst in Cuba during 1998 recording this 'Master Sessions Series'.

3. Eliot, T. S, *The Complete Poems and Plays*, FOUR QUAR-TETS, Faber and Faber Ltd, 1969, p. 186.

4. Humboldt, Alexander Von, *Personal Narrative Of A Journey To The Equinoctial Regions Of The New Continent*, Penguin Classics, 1995 edition, p. 95.

5. Humboldt, Alexander Von, *Personal Narrative Of A Journey To The Equinoctial Regions Of The New Continent*, Penguin Classics, 1995 edition, p. 280.

6. Hemingway, Ernest, *THE OLD MAN AND THE SEA*, Arrow Books, 1993, p.79.

7. Eliot, T. S, *The Complete Poems and Plays*, FOUR QUAR-TETS, Faber and Faber Ltd, 1969, p. 184.

8. Brathwaite, Edward, *THE ARRIVANTS*, Oxford University Press, 1973, pp. 212 - 213.

9. Eliot, T. S, *The Complete Poems and Plays*, FOUR QUAR-TETS, Faber and Faber Ltd, 1969, p. 186.

10. Eliot, T. S, *The Complete Poems and Plays*, FOUR QUAR-TETS, Faber and Faber Ltd, 1969, p. 187.

11. *Vientos Alisios*: Trade Winds, as referred to by Christopher Columbus in his Diaries.

12. Humboldt, Alexander Von, *Personal Narrative Of A Journey To The Equinoctial Regions Of The New Continent*, Penguin Classics, 1995 edition, Introduction, p. XLViii.

13. Humboldt, Alexander Von, *Personal Narrative Of A Journey To The Equinoctial Regions Of The New Continent*, Penguin Classics, 1995 edition, p. 95.

14. Eliot, T. S, *The Complete Poems and Plays*, FOUR QUAR-TETS, Faber and Faber Ltd, 1969, p. 197.

15. Brathwaite, Edward, *THE ARRIVANTS*, Oxford University Press, 1973, p 184.

16. Brathwaite, Edward, *THE ARRIVANTS*, Oxford University Press, 1973, pp. 265 - 266.

17. Conrad, Joseph, *THE HEART OF DARKNESS*, Everyman, 1967, pp. 32 - 33.

18. *Magnetic North and Geographical North*: Christopher Columbus was the first person to ever note this difference

and to compensate for it - a great achievement for a time that preceded intense open-Sea navigation.

19. Entry in the *Diary* of Christopher Columbus for Saturday 22nd September, 1492. Translated from the Spanish by the author.

20. *Thanks be to God for the trade winds:* translation from the Spanish.

21. This is what Christopher Columbus wrote of Cuba. It was also the first mention of the Island of Cuba by him in his Diary. He also wrote on Saturday 20th - Sunday 21st October, 1492 that: '*Everything is so green and so beautiful that I do not know how one could ever depart from here*'.

22. Eliot, T. S, *The Complete Poems and Plays*, Rhapsody on a Windy Night, Faber and Faber Ltd, 1969, p. 24.

23. ST. JOHN THE DIVINE, *THE REVELATION OF*, Chapter 10, The New Testament.
The author visited the tomb of St. John the Divine in Selçuk, Turkey.

The forthcoming release by 'Up, Bustle and Out'

- an abstract of a proposed new album, fusing film and literature for release in 2002

...Bohemia...
- former kingdoms speak

This release combines music and film in equal proportions. The documentation will take place between Berlin and Istanbul where the land journey will be captured on 16mm and Super 8 film. Recording sessions with solo instrumentalists and full orchestras will be both organised and open to chance encounters.

The songs 'Telegraph Poles' and 'Stereo Literati' we hope to engage Yugoslav cult film director Emir Kusturica's 'No Smoking Orchestra' for some weird and wonderful studio session recordings.

At least half the album will be taken to Eastern Europe, as backing tracks on professional recording equipment, in search of undiscovered and wild talent. The recordings will then be edited and mastered in our Bristol studio.

This album will be the 6th by Up, Bustle and Out and a radical departure from previous material. The production will be atmospheric, the songs moodier, the instruments rarer - such as Russian theremins, Hungarian strings, reedy oboes, disembodied voices....

Double bass will be played by Jim Barr of 'Portishead', saxophones by Martin Genge and Vicky Burke, trumpet by Andy Hague, and harmonica by Keith Warmington. We also aim to feature the photographic finesse of award winning Ljalja Kuznetsova - famous for her portraits of Gypsy life, contrasted by Simon Marsden's Eastern European ghost and landscape photography.

'Waldo Films' founder Mr Julian Elvins will, hopefully, be shooting, splicing, fragmenting and presenting the final film accompaniments. He will be working on this with Rudolf Mustdagh, director of 'Lock, Stock and 2 Smoking Barrels', as screened on Channel 4.

Desired formats: DVD, CD and CD-ROM and a Vinyl double album.

Extras: Collage pullout and an edited book from our pub-lishing imprint 'la prensa rebelde' relating the adventures encountered en-route towards the ancient city of Istanbul where the land journey shall finish.

Promotion: Dub-plate mixing on 4 decks of our studio ses-sions, Percussion, Flamenco guitar, full-size film projections and stage banners, book extract readings and discussions.

World-wide web: www.upbustleandout.co.uk
Detailing: discography, updates, film, music, gallery, literary publications, news, gigs....

Up, Bustle and Out - to ears hooped in gold
                                                 are heard rumours rumbling the
                                                 open roads

From the **British** reviews of **Master Sessions 1, Calle 23, Havana** and **The Rebel Radio Diary**

Venue Magazine, 4-18 August oo, Bristol, UK
The Rebel Radio Diary
Rupert Mould (La Prensa Rebelde)

'The Rebel Radio Diary', explains the writer in the early pages of these chronicles of his time in Cuba, 'is an emotional and often direct observation, intending also to be historical, humorous, real, fantastical, romantic and, above all, captured through the aperture of youth. But Rupert Mould's travels on this most fascinating of islands are no mere sightseeing expeditions; he's not just another travel writer on a rather pleasurable junket, his words serving to solely (and briefly) entertain the chattering classes as they flick through their Sunday newspapers. No, Mould has a clear purpose, he's a man on a mission. As the visionary force behind Bristolian music collective 'Up, Bustle & Out', he's off to Cuba not only to deliver equipment and CDs to Radio Rebelde (the radio station originally set up by Che Guevara), but also to gather together some of Cuba's finest musicians and stick them in a studio to record their contributions to a future UB&O album.

And, before anyone suggests that Ry Cooder got there first, Mould's travels were made well before the Buena Vista Social Club project was unleashed upon the world. And, while the million-selling project concentrated almost exclusively on the performers and their stories of past glories, Mould digs deeper into the Cuban psyche, telling an unashamedly political story of the daily struggle of life on the island. With the recordings safely in the can, Mould grabs his backpack and criss-crosses Cuba on clanking trains and overcrowded buses. While what he sees and encounters is keenly informed by his sharp take on historical events, there's also a charm and partial naivety underlying his adventures. Like Graham Greene before him (whose spirit is very apparent within these pages), he's an Englishman abroad, albeit one, as he states, seeing things 'through the aperture of youth'. And this shapes the diary, presenting a very honest and personal account of his experiences and his predictions forCuba's future.

It's clear that Mould feels an instant and emotional link with the island and its citizens who, despite forty-odd years of American aggression and embargoes that affect every Cuban every day, are painted as very proud and (largely) very welcoming people. They are tremendously poor but they are not peasants. Let us remember, as a quote from The Guardian's Jonathan Glancey reminds us, that Miami, Havana's ugly, unidentical twin, is permanently scarred by crime, illiteracy, drugs and violence whilst the Cuban capital is one of grace and culture, its population dignified, well-educated and law-abiding. Rupert Mould's diary builds on Glancey's words, paying a reverential tribute - no, a homage - to a society that has shown extraordinary resilience in the face of extreme intimidation. For a study of humanity that's both poetic and polemical, you should read it. Nige Tassell

The Independent On Sunday, Discs Of The Week, 23 July 2000
UP, BUSTLE AND OUT
Rebel Radio
Master Sessions 1 (Ninja Tune)
In 1997, Bristol-based beatmakers Up, Bustle & Out released a single to commemorate the 30th anniversary of Che Guevara's death, donating the proceeds to Radio Rebelde, the radio station he founded. In return, they were invited to Cuba to make a record with Richard Egües (who's billed as Cuba's number one flautist) and his rhythm section. The result is this multimedia project – the CD includes a CD-ROM with three short films, and there's a book out too – of which the best bit by far is the music. Breakbeats and drum 'n' bass mingle with Cuban rhythms whilst British sampling technology gets to grips with traditional instruments and fragments of rousing communist rhetoric. It's a credit to both parties that the fusion is not just successful, but fresh and fun too. LP

U, B &O are great but these remixes take them to another level! Snowboy & PhD mixes - brilliant. (Andy Smith - Portishead - worldwide)

DJ PROMOTIONAL SUMMARY
UB&O seem to have got the balance right on this one and it's working on the dance-floor as well as appealing in bars and at home. Fantastic reactions across the board. The ideas and the effort behind the album have won them a lot of fans, and now there's a tangible buzz and desire out there for them. (Duncan Smith, ZZonked Promotions, London)

Muzik Magazine, Album Of The Issue, July 2000
UP, BUSTLE & OUT
Rebel Radio Master Sessions 1, (Ninja Tune)
WHEN UP, Bustle & Out make an album they don't mess
about. When they talk of making a Bristol meets Cuba
record, they don't simply grab a riff from some old Cuban
track and smoke a few cigars for effect. No, this is the
real deal. Teaming up with Richard Egües – Cuba's number one flautist and orchestrator – this is music-making
that truly honours the spirit of Cuba. Mould and D. 'Ein'
Fell don't just leave it at the music either. There's a movie
and a book to boot. Slices of Jules Elvin's faded Super 8
documentary-style film and excerpts from their Rebel
Radio Diary are included on the CD.

   But what of the music itself? Let's not beat about the
bush. This album is superb. 'Hip Hop Barrio' rocks out
with funk as deep as the Grand Canyon and rollercoaster-
steep drum builds, while 'Rebel Satellite', is a mouth-
organ-fest with one seriously funky drummer and some
sinister electronic twists. When you add to those the laid-
back soul of 'Por Eso Quiero', the darkly minimal
'Havana's Streets', and the docu-drama composition
'Kennedy's Secret Tapes', about the Cuban invasion,
you've got an album and a half. Compelling, beautiful and
hip-shudderingly funky, we can't wait for Sessions 2.
Susanna Glaser.

The Guardian Newspaper
THIS WEEK'S ESSENTIAL RELEASES
POP
UP, BUSTLE & OUT Rebel Radio Master Sessions (Ninja
Tune ZENCD46)

British clubland's fascination with Latin and Brazilian sounds continues to grow. The Cuban interests of Bristol's Up ,Bustle & Out posse led to their 1997 tribute to Che Guevara, which in turn led to an invitation to record in Havana, where they worked with master flautist Richard Egües. Rebel Radio mixes the resultant swaying Descargas with UBO's Seventies funk, breakbeats and samples. The result is an impressionist musical diary, supported by movie footage for your computer and an imminent published travelogue. All in all, just the kind of intriguing madcap project which no Major label would dream of funding.

The Big Issue Magazine, July 10-16 2000
ALBUM OF THE WEEK
UP, BUSTLE & OUT
Rebel Radio Master Sessions 1
(Ninja Tune)
This is a tribute to Che Guevara's revolutionary radio station 'Radio Rebelde'. Recorded in Cuba with the help of Cuban flautist Richard Egües and, presumably Fidel Castro, Rebel Radio...also features new and archive CD-ROM Super 8 footage of Havana, edited to the music. There's even a Guevara diaries-aping book on the way. The music backs up these lofty aspirations. Dense, humid, breaks-based funk – you'd call it jungle if that name wasn't already taken.

DJ mag, August 2000
Up, Bustle & Out
Rebel Radio Master Sessions 1 Ninja Tune
In 1997 Up, Bustle & Out released an EP in memory of
Che Guevara on the 30th anniversary of his death. They
also donated tour and recording royalties to the Che
Guevara founded Radio Rebelde radio station. Together
these two gestures led to a rare invitation from some of
Cuba's finest musicians to come and record in Cuba. The
result is the Rebel Radio Sessions 1, an album which suc-
cessfully marries Bristolian beat culture with traditional
Cuban rhythms. If you think this could sound somewhat
contrived, check this album and prepare to be more than
pleasantly surprised.   9/10 Dan Irwin

From the **American** reviews

Stern's Music, Brazil.
So I was very pleased to notice a couple of months ago
that a new U, B & O CD, 'Rebel Radio Vol. 1' is due out
on 'Ninja'. We still have inquiries today about U, B & O
as a result of the tracks on our Brazilian compilation.
I was even more pleased when I saw the single has
remixes by 'Smith & Mighty' [whose work I also really
like]. So far I have only heard 'Hip Hop Barrio' from the
Ninja Sampler CD. So you can imagine I am thoroughly
looking forward to hearing some of the other new material – especially with the CD having been recorded in Cuba.
The world will be a better place as a result.
Cheers,
Paul @ Stern's Music, Brazil.

BPM culture, djmixed.com, USA, October 2000
Up, Bustle and Out; The Rebel Radio Diary
...Sometimes recording an album that involves artists from completely different backgrounds can lead to a bitter, forgetful experience. Mould's accounts of travel to Cuba are quite optimistic, even during periods of extreme complication. The travelogue describes the long wait at customs, the fear of losing expensive, donated equipment, and the vast differences between two cultures. These descriptions never overshadow the task at hand, which is to complete a well-planned project while evading the sinister spectre of failure. By reading the accounts of this experience one can truly appreciate an album that respects craftsmanship, while focusing intently on further innovation.

During a long process and much planning the Rebel Radio project took place in two differing countries, accessible only to those that had the similar need to make music from the heart. After procuring visas, funding, donations and contacts in Cuba, Rupert makes his way to discover a country surviving on it's own, though plagued by foreign sanctions. He tells of a population that views its own situation as one of complete freedom, one that is savored.

The Rebel Radio Diary is an important account of how a project is completed from beginning to end. It is essential in helping us to understand the many details of the recording process, contractual obligations, and frustrations that may occur. It also weaves a tale of someone who is so dedicated to his craft, and respectful of the sacrifice others have made allowing him to visit their country and collaborate with them, producing music that can be passed on through generations.

If you are not familiar with the previous works of Up, Bustle and Out, you should start with this book. When accompanied by the album it will demonstrate the current technological advances of film, CD ROM and post-production techniques giving insight to the making of several of the songs, as well as showing the internal beauty of a country that few will get a chance to experience. The Author has experienced many cultures, made countless acquaintances, and made memorable music. If only he could muster the time and energy to document every recording in a similar way. (Jon Wesley)

TIME OUT NEW YORK
New York, NY
Aug 10, 2000
Up, Bustle and Out
Rebel Radio: Master Sessions 1, Calle 23, Havana (Ninja Tune)

The predominant mediocre musical sound in clubs at the moment is a bland, pseudomulticultural mélange of funky beats, cocktail jazz and any of a number of watered-down international styles, mainly African or Latin in nature. The whole thing might be made up to sound like a hip, old soundtrack. This music is generally innocuous, not unpleasant on the ears, and devoid of anything resembling a soul – and it must be easy to make, because there's assloads of it out right now. It's a result of a conceit that's been spreading recently: that anything in the world sounds good with a catchy beat behind it.

The two worldly English cats who comprise Up, Bustle and Out have what it takes to make this kind of music work: an easygoing nature, a sense for the spirit of the music they're mixing with their spy-movie soundtrack fare, and a delicate touch in the studio. Rebel Radio Master Sessions 1 came about because the duo, Rupert Mould (dubbed "Señor Roody" for this record) and Ein (who takes the name "Clandestine" here), released an EP in 1997 observing the 30th anniversary of Che Guevara's death. Later, the pair donated some equipment to Cuba's Radio Rebelde, and that led to an invitation to record in Havana with Richard Egües, an orchestrator and flautist who appears on two of the Buena Vista Social Club records.

What Señor Roody and Ein get right is the realization that their cool, laid-back beats and the varying traditional Cuban forms provided by Egües and his orquesta have more in common in terms of vibe than in sound. So rather than merely pasting one to the other and making a pan-Atlantic mess, they've composed a record that glides between the styles, letting moods play off each other and slipping in suggestive samples of radical radio dialogue for effect. Roody and Ein might be playing it a little too safe at times, but they nail the formula perfectly on "Carbine 744, 520...Che Guevara," where a guitarist named Cuffy "El Guapo" weaves a Flamenco line through all manners of funky beats, and the two sides – Havana, Cuba, and Bristol, England – play musical tag with each other.

Another great summer record.

- Mike Wolf

PULSE
West Sacramento, CA, October, 2000
Up Bustle and Out
Presents Rebel Radio Master Sessions, Calle 23, Havana
(Ninja Tune)
   Capitalizing on the Cuban craze, Up, Bustle and Out hit
Elian's little island, resulting in this groundbreaking trip-
hop / salsa melting pot. With flautist Richard Egües of
Buena Vista Social Club conducting the all-Havana recording sessions, the UBO trio mesh the romance, rhythms
and cigar smoke of the Communist colony with their
swank Bristol beats and cut-up technology. Most tunes
assimilate native styles, draping fragment sounds with
UBO's clever sampledelia, but there are also stretches of
pure Habana riffing and rolling. Kennedy, Castro and Che
Guevara also drop in, the politicos' warlike remarks
framed in time over beats, tobacco and tunes. The lushly
packaged CD / CD-ROM also contains a Havana travelogue
of both the old and new city, footage of the recording
sessions and info on the original Rebel Radio, founded by
old Che himself back in '58 (and still broadcasting today).
This is the future sound of Cuba. ****
                                          - Ken Micallef

CMJ NEW MUSIC MONTHLY
New York, NY, October 2000
REVOLUTIONARY CUBAN
Up, Bustle And Out ain't no Buena Vista Social Club.
Call it the curse of the Buena Vista Social Club. Soon
after the acid-jazz group Up, Bustle And Out finished its
summit with a studio of Cuban musicians – which result-

ed in Master Sessions 1, Calle 23, Havana (Ninja Tune) –
Buena Vista mania overtook NPR. For those happy to cap-
italize on trends, the phenomena might seem like a bless-
ing, but the Bristol-based members of UB&O worried that
music fans wouldn't accept their unorthodox approach to
Cuban music after falling in love with Buena Vista Social
Club's reverent son.

"They worked so hard to keep things pure," says Up,
Bustle and Out honcho and in-house philosopher Rupert
Mould about Ry Cooder's all-star band. "We didn't want
to do that. We didn't want to record anything that had
been done before."

Mould's hands-on work with Cuban music dates back to
1997, when UB&O recorded A Dream Of Land And
Freedom, an EP that honored the 30th anniversary of Che
Guevara's death. After the members of UB&O donated the
proceeds from the single to the state-run Sonocaribe
Studio where they recorded it, the Cuban government
invited them back to continue experimenting.

"I definitely wanted to play with a sound that was remi-
niscent of the Cuban descarga of the 1950s," says Mould
of his trip-hop-meets-guajira creations. "The studio and
the equipment, all the old valves, reflected that – a more
traditional sound." The union of lo-fi tech and wheezing
instruments is alternately breezy and bouncy, but always
laid-back, whether UB&O is reproducing traditional vocal
and flute lines verbatim or layering hip-hop beats with
ballpark organs and vibes.

Master Sessions is less a nostalgic flashback than an
era-hopping volley between Up, Bustle and Out's break-
beat internationalism, Afro-Cuban drumming, sampled
radio broadcasts from Radio Rebelde and an intergenera-

tional squad of Cuban descarga players assembled by ex-
Orquesta Aragon flautist Richard Egües (who also helped
organize the Buena Vista Social Club). The cultural colli-
sions left such an impression on Mould, an erstwhile aca-
demic, that he turned his experiences as a Brit in Cuba
into a first-person travelogue, The Rebel Radio Diary (La
Prensa Rebelde).

Explains Mould, "I was involved with the musicians but
I was also just walking around and viewing, seeing the
people and the culture and putting it together with the
country's history. I never saw myself as an outsider. I was
there enjoying a rare moment in the life of the country."
Josh Kun

AP. ALTERNATIVE PRESS MAGAZINE, INC.
Volume 15, Number 149, December 2000
Up, Bustle and Out, Master Sessions 1

Dancing around politics in Havana.

Cuba's musical heritage, a source of periodic fascination
and inspiration for Northern fans and audiences, has
come back into vogue of late, thanks largely to the suc-
cess of the Buena Vista Social Club and their offshoots.
The newest addition to the Cuban revival comes from Up,
Bustle and Out, well-established Bristol trip-hoppers, who
enlisted the help of Social Club collaborator Richard
Egües for these Havana recordings. The product of those
sessions, the album alternates between breaks-driven
numbers and the more fluid orchestral stylings of traditional Cuban music. The music is pleasant enough, but it

fails to go very far – the downtempo tracks seem dated, fusing dusty breaks and spy movie music in a kind of by-the numbers trip hop, and the orchestral Cuban songs don't really approximate the energy attained on the Buena Vista Social Club recordings. Most troubling, though, is the Cold War rhetoric that frames the release, complete with "secret transmissions" and references to "spying, leaked documents, romantic revolutionaries, cigar scandals, beautiful agents with falsified passports and secretly taped high-level conversations." Without a real sense of history, or a compelling formal context, the rhetoric seems like an empty gesture – politics as fashion – that ultimately trivializes the whole project. (Philip Sherburne).

Subject: Afterschool Hip Hop Culture Program
Date: Thu, 16 Nov 2000 12:31:38 -0800
From: "Los Angeles Centre for Education Research (LACER)"
sstricke@lausd.k12.ca.us

I am writing to let you know about an After-school pro-gram that I teach. I teach Hip Hop Culture to middle school students through the LACER STARS After-school Program.

In short, the Los Angeles Centre for Education Research (LACER) is a non-profit organization that operates after-school programs in four middle schools in the Hollywood area. Each program gets about 100 students per day, 99% of whom qualify for the federal free, or reduced lunch program. I teach Hip Hop Culture - a class that attempts to not only get them dancing and breakin', but also educates them on the positives of Hip Hop. My goal is to give our students options, to get them to challenge and question the world around them, particularly what music they see on MTV and hear on commercial radio.

Artists who have come through my program are people like Cut Chemist (Jurassic 5ive) and Miles Tackett (Breakestra), Saul Williams, DJ Irene (for a li'l House music education), and Garth Trinidad (KCRW radio).

I'm a huge fan of UP, BUSTLE & OUT and I would LOVE to receive copies to share with my students.

I look forward to speaking with you.
Sincerely,
Joe Hernandez-Kolski